More Tellable Cracker Tales

More
Tellable Cracker Tales

Annette J. Bruce

PINEAPPLE PRESS, INC., Sarasota, Florida

This one is dedicated to my four grand-Crackers—Amy, Bruce, David, and Joe—all of whom, on their own, made Florida their home!

In Appreciation
I would like to acknowledge my indebtedness and express my appreciation to David and June Cussen and Kris Rowland of Pineapple Press, the many helpful librarians, and the historians, storytellers, and friends who have contributed much to *More Tellable Cracker Tales.*
—Annette J. Bruce

Inquiries should be addressed to:

Pineapple Press, Inc.
P.O. Box 3889
Sarasota, Florida 34230
www.pineapplepress.com

Library of Congress Cataloging-in-Publication Data

Bruce, Annette J.
    More tellable cracker tales / Annette J. Bruce.— 1st ed.
        p.   cm.
    Includes index.
    ISBN 1-56164-253-3 (alk. paper) — ISBN 1-56164-256-8 (pbk. : alk. paper)
        I. Title.

GR110.F5 B778 2002
398'.09759—dc21

                                                                                2002025128

First Edition
10 9 8 7 6 5 4 3 2 1

Design by Carol Tornatore
Composition by Shé Sicks
Printed in the United States of America

Contents

Preface

One of my life's greatest pleasures is to read of this great state's past. It becomes even more delightful when one can do this through the eyes of those who actually lived in those days gone by. This collection of stories, gathered and retold by Annette Bruce, is done in the language and thoughts of those who have provided us this window into what and who made Florida unique. It provides one not familiar with our history a unique insight into the Florida of yesteryear.

In reviewing this collection, I have found hours of laughter and, more importantly, another look into my state's colorful past. I am sure you will find as much and more.

Everett A. Kelly
Representative, District 42
Florida House of Representatives

Introduction

As I reflect on the stories in *More Tellable Cracker Tales*, I become aware that some of the stories in this volume might be classified as leftovers, in as much as I was telling them before *Tellable Cracker Tales* went to press. The word "leftovers" reminds me of my friend's husband, who disliked being served leftover food. One evening my friend had nothing on the dinner table except leftovers. Her husband sat down and started eating.

My friend chided him a little. "Honey," she said, "aren't you going to ask the blessing?"

"Show me one thing on this table that hasn't already been blessed, and I'll be happy to" he replied and continued to feed his face.

I'll admit that only some foods and marriages are better the second time around, but all stories improve with the telling. As each person is unique, each story is different and creates its own reason for existing. And each time a story is told it will be a little different because different tellers are telling it and assuredly because different listeners are hearing it.

The title of this offering of tellable tales has caused no small stir. One of the many who questioned me concerning the name "Cracker" asked me if I would not feel insulted if someone called me a "Cracker." After I told him I would not in any way feel insulted, he remarked, "I guess it would depend on who called you a Cracker." But I quickly assured him that anyone who wanted to insult me would have to call me something other than a "Florida Cracker"! As "class" has little to do with wealth or worldly possessions—graciousness is a key ingredient—I am convinced that the nineteenth-century Florida Crackers were folks with class, worthy of emulation.

Each story in this book was chosen and tailored with not only the reader/teller in mind but the listener as well. Without hesitation, I recommend that your bookshelf and your repertoire include both *Tellable Cracker Tales* and *More Tellable Cracker Tales.*

—Annette J. Bruce

Introduction
Cracker Jack Tales

While the core of the Cracker Jack story is deeply rooted in Southern folklore, Cracker Jack is a character I created to personify the humor and values of native Floridians as I have observed them for more than three-quarters of a century.

The Florida Jack, like the Appalachian Jack, is a popular character who can—and usually does—enjoy a bushel of fun while stirring up a peck of trouble. Cracker Jack tales are short, easy to learn, and enjoy the same wide appeal of the Appalachian Jack tales. Thus, Cracker Jack stories make wonderful fillers, which are often a godsend to a storyteller. Remember to keep them simple and uncluttered—much of their humor depends upon their brevity.

Do Tell!

Cracker Jack's Education

C racker Jack, like many of his peers, was smarter in the head than the Yankees thought him to be. Even his Yankee teacher thought little of Jack's learning. This was to Jack's liking, for he never could figure out no reason atall for being in sech an all-fired hurry to get into the next grade. Why, every time you'd get into another grade, they'd expect you to learn a lot of new stuff. So, Jack was fifteen years old and still in the fifth grade.

One day his teacher wrote on the blackboard, and then read aloud the sentence, "I ain't had no fun atall dis here whole summer long." Then she asked Jack what she should do to correct this.

After some serious thought, Jack said, "Well, I reckon you might start out by gettin' yoreself a feller."

This embarrassed the teacher. She gave Jack a sheet of paper and a dictionary and said, "Go to the back of the room and write this sentence in your own words: 'A spasmodic movement of the optic is as adequate as a slight inclination of the cranium to an equine corrupted and devoid of his visionary capacity'."

Jack said, "Please, Miss, run that one past me one more time."

The teacher said, "I've written it on this piece of paper. See? 'A spasmodic movement of the optic is as adequate as a slight inclination of the cranium to an equine corrupted and devoid of his visionary capacity.'"

"Now, Miss Crenshaw," drawled Cracker Jack, "I'm jest a cracker, but I shore don't need no dictionary, nor none of them fifty-cent words neither, to know that a wink is as good as a nod to a blind hoss."

Telling time: 3–4 minutes
Audience: 5th grade–adult

Prior to the twentieth century, the interior of Florida was sparsely populated. Public libraries and schools of higher learning were as scarce as hen's teeth. Because of their isolation, many of Florida's citizens made an effort to stay informed about world events. They eagerly welcomed and conversed with the occasional traveler, and they read and re-read every word of newspapers that were weeks, sometimes months, old. This situation produced a class of people whose speech was not governed by any rules of grammar or syntax but was often generously sprinkled with erudite words.

A Few Simple Questions

C racker Jack retained his penchant for fun and frolic long after his peers had settled into rocking chairs. Tickled by the many exaggerated accounts of how Florida's climate would add years to your life, Cracker Jack was looking forward to the expected visit of the Yankee census-taker.

Down on his knees in the front yard shooting marbles, Jack sat back on his heels and called off the dogs when the caller came to the gate.

The man uneasily shifted his briefcase to his left hand and cleared his throat. "I'm with the U.S. Department of Statistics. Is there anyone here who could answer a few simple questions for me?"

"Right now, I'm the only one here, but you must be livin' right, 'cause yore luck is shore with ye! I'm so good at answerin' simple questions they call me Simple Jack."

"Do you live here?"

"I reckon I do. I ain't dead here."

"How old are you?"

"I'll celebrate my sixteenth birthday comes the twenty-ninth of February."

"February only has twenty-eight days except in leap year."

"Yes, sir. That's what they tell me. Iffen I weren't one of those leapin' babies, I'd be a whole lot older."

"Are you telling me that you are sixty-three years of age?"

"No, sir. It's easier for me ter just keep up with my birthdays. You can figure out my age for yoreself."

"Does anyone else live here?"

"Right now, jest me and my pa."

"Where is he?"

"My pa? He's pickin' oranges today."

"Picking oranges!" the census-taker uttered in total disbelief. "How old is he?"

"He was ninety, January fifteenth past."

"And just the two of you live here?"

"Yes, sir. Ma got mad at Pa 'cause he kept flirtin' with the new schoolmarm and went home to her mama. And I reckon Grandpa won't be livin' here no more either."

"No, I guess your grandpa is dead."

"Well, you've guessed wrong, mister. He just left here this morning goin' to the justice of the peace to get married."

"Your grandpa is getting married?"

"I'm afraid he is!"

"How old is he?"

"We celebrated his one hundred twelfth birthday last Sunday."

"Now, what on earth would a hundred-and-twelve-year-old man want to get married for?"

"Oh, he didn't want to—they're makin' him. It's one of 'em shotgun weddings, and Grandpa knows that Betty Lou's pa is the best shot in this neck of the woods. So you can count on Grandpa being married by the time that Florida sun sinks into that lake."

Telling time: 6–7 minutes
Audience: adults

In the eighteenth and nineteenth centuries, tuberculosis ran rampant in the northern states. When it was found that Florida's climate was a miracle cure for the dreaded disease, real estate hawkers made the most of this selling point. The stories about the healing properties of Florida's climate were embellished until they were beyond belief by even the most naive, but these tall tales were especially enjoyed by the teller with an uninitiated listener.

The Storm of Storms

Cracker Jack was well liked by most folks, even those who believed him to be downright lazy. Others better understood Jack and knew that his primary problem was his notion. You see, he had a notion that life was one big party and that it was his sacred duty to enjoy it.

Today was Saturday and Jack's birthday, which gave vent to his notion. Jack was up bright and early getting his chores done so that he could get on with the business of having fun. Before he had finished feeding up, he spied his Grandpa riding up, leading his young white mule, Buncombe.

As you might have guessed, it was the family's admiration of Col. William Harney that had promoted the unusual name for the mule, and Cracker Jack thought that even Harney's horse couldn't be any smarter than his Grandpa's mule, so he couldn't believe his good fortune when he heard his Grandpa say, "Take good care of her, son! Have a happy birthday and many more. Yore Grandma and I love ya!"

After a hearty breakfast, Jack got his Saturday night's bath Saturday morning and put on the new clothes his ma and pa had given him. He slicked back his hair and, sitting proudly on the back of his mule, started out for Micanopy. It being Saturday, the horseshoe pitching, checker playing, and bragging would be in rare form around Veaseley's Store; so Cracker Jack was in high spirits.

As he rode down the road, he hailed Monk Martin, who was plowing his garden.

"Why, Jack," said Monk, "you're dressed up like you're goin' ter preachin'."

This challenged Jack to convince the old, hard-working, illiterate farmer that today was Sunday. "Why, of course, Mr. Monk, I'm on my way to church. Purtin-nigh fell offen Buncombe here when I seed you out plowin' on the Sabbath Day."

"Sabbath? Aw, Jack, you're jest a-jawin' me. Today is Saturday."

"No, Mr. Monk, I hate to tell you this, but you have done lost a day sommers. Today is Sunday, and if I wuz you I'd unhitch 'at mule and get back to the house 'fore the preacher comes 'long. Why, he'll condemn your soul to hell for sure iffen he sees you a-plowin' on Sunday."

"Yeah, I reckon he would," Monk said and started unhitching his mule, and Jack rode on, singing "Shall We Gather at the River."

Monk Martin started back toward his house. When he was within hearing distance, he called to his wife, "Molly, get them clothes back in the house 'fore someone sees you out here washin' on Sunday."

"Monk, have you tuk leave of yore senses? Today is Saturday!"

"Yeah, that's what you said, and had me out there plowin' when Cracker Jack came 'long all dressed up—a-goin' ter preachin'."

Monk caught and killed a big fat hen, and Molly cooked it with dumplings and the fixings. They ate a big dinner and sat around all day. Can't say that they prayed or even conversed with each other, because they were too worried-up over being a day behind with their work.

The next morning when the sun came up, the Martins were already up, champin' at the bit to get to their duties. Monk hitched up the mule and had almost finished plowing the garden and Molly was up to her elbows in lye soap when the preacher pulled up in his buggy.

"Monk Martin, I've long suspected that you were a man who had sold his soul to the devil. You frequently rob the Lord of time that belongs to Him by missing church services and have insisted on your wife doing likewise, but I never thought that even you were such a blatant sinner that you would actually plow on the Sabbath." He continued to deliver one of his most powerful fire-and-brimstone sermons.

Monk doffed his hat and stood there scratching his head before he spoke. "Preacher, what you've been sayin' ain't changed me much, but I've been 'round for more 'an fifty years and never have I seed sech weather as we've been havin' here lately. That storm we had t'other day wus the worst one I ever seed. When it lightened up and I came outten the house ter see the damages, there wus so much water in the yard that I knowed right away that the storm had blowed both of my wells clean outten the ground. Of course, they got so much water in them that they finally sunk back down. The next mornin', I found that that ole crooked road that used to wind its way down to the waterin' hole—well, Preacher, that storm had blowed that crooked road as straight as an arrow. And now I'm findin' out that it's done mixed up the days of the week so dreadful that we got two Sundays back ter back. I tell you, it's 'nough to make a body think 'bout changin' his ways, 'cause they jest ain't no tellin' what else that storm did or when 'nother one will come along more devilish than that storm of storms we jest had!"

Telling time: 8–9 minutes
Audience: 5th grade–adult

This story could be used as a springboard to learn more about William Selby Harney, America's most unsung hero. He was in Florida when he got his first commission in the U.S. Army. He did much of his fighting in Florida and made his home in Orlando at the time of his death. During his lifetime, the Indians called him a native name that meant "man who runs like a deer." At his death, they changed his name to "man who always keeps his word." He was often referred to as "the Indians' friendliest foe." He served as both Jefferson Davis's and Abraham Lincoln's commanding officer during their stints in the Army. Lincoln greatly admired Harney.

Lake Harney in central Florida and the Harney River in south Florida were named to honor him. There are a number of other geographical points and at least one town in the West that also bear his name. Yet most Americans have never heard of William Selby Harney.

And, by the way, they may not have heard of his horse, Buncombe, either. In their day William Harney and Buncombe were as well known as Roy Rogers and Trigger.

Introduction
Folktales and Legends

While readers will find the stories in this category full of interest, the teller will find it a mother lode. "A Vanishing Breed" may be told as written or as three different short stories. The story lines of "The Legend of Bernice and Claire" and "The Indian Legend of Florida's Silver Springs" are similar, and it has been said that the legend of Bernice and Claire is just a more elaborate tale of the ancient Indian legend. Since many disappointed or frustrated lovers have sought death together rather than live apart, both legends might be founded on truth. The legend of Bernice and Claire was declared to be the unvarnished truth by many of the old residents of Silver Springs, and Aunt Silla, who lived into the twentieth century, related the part she played in the drama many times.

If told with zest, "Jumbo Jim," "Mastodon Hunt," "Marooning on the Matanzas," and "Whirlwind" can hold older children and adults spellbound.

Do Tell!

A Vanishing Breed

A Florida backcountry woman was hoeing out beside her weather-beaten house. A neighbor stopped and leaned on the fence. "Effie Mae," she said, "it ain't fittin' for you to be hoein' out here today when the whole town knows that you jest had a letter from the government sayin' that yore Jim is layin' out in one of them furrin heathen lands, dead! It just ain't fittin'."

Effie Mae rested her hoe and looked at her neighbor with level eyes. "Friend," she said, "I know you mean well, but you just don't understand. This is Jim's land, and it rejoiced his heart to see green things growin' because it meant that the young'uns and me would be eatin'. This is his hoe, and when I'm hoein', I can feel his strong arms around me and his big hands on mine, and hear his voice sayin', 'That's good, Maw. That's good!' I can't afford a stone monument for Jim—wished I could—but workin', not weepin', is the only headstone I can give him. So if you don't mind, neighbor, I'll do my grievin' in my own way."

When I read this little gem in the newspaper, I folded the paper and dropped it into my lap. I sat there thinking about how the dirt farmers of yesteryear were often called hayseeds, clodhoppers, and country bumpkins, but they always held a real fascination for me. These rugged individuals had a certain earthiness about their thinking and a way of expressing it that, to me, were both amusing and refreshing.

My friend's father, Roy, was no exception. He lived on the old family farm close to Bunnell. Kate, his wife of forty years, died the week following the attack on Pearl Harbor. My friend wanted her father to sell the farm and move to Jacksonville, where his life could be a little easier, but Roy didn't "cotton to that notion atall." A weekend in the city was as much as he could "stomach." Besides, his country was at war. He couldn't do any of the actual fighting, but he could still grow food for those who did.

The last time I saw Roy, the thought occurred to me that it might be our last visit. Wishing I could have the story of his life, I asked him to tell me about some of the folks he had known. He looked at me for a few moments. His tired, old eyes gradually brightened. He got rid of his "cud" and said, "Well, durin' the Depression our place got tagged by professional hobos and tramps, and, of course, some just down-and-outers stopped by too. Never a week went by that we didn't have a dozen or more wanting handouts. Kate—bless her heart—was always too kind for her own good. On the farms we had food enough to spare, but one evenin' when Kate was fixin' food for the fourth one that day, I got to thinkin', Why should my wife work, and then cook and clean up after them who didn't? There was always something needin' to be done 'round the farm, and if they wanted to eat, they could work for it. So I told Kate, 'Enough is enough. From now on, no one eats unless he works.' It wasn't long before this decision thinned out the number lookin' for handouts at our place.

"One evenin', about sundown, a cold northwester started blowin' in. After Kate finished in the kitchen, I put another log on the fire, and we pulled our chairs up a little closer to the fireplace. We was listenin' to the radio and shellin' pecans when the dogs started barkin' and someone outside started squawkin'. I went to the door and there was a stranger askin' for a meal. He was better dressed and cleaner than most, and so I was plumb confounded when he grabbed up that ax and started splittin' that wood like lightning, and he didn't let up till he had laid in more wood than the box would hold. Kate and me noticed that he washed his hands and bowed his head to give thanks before he ate.

"'Stranger,' I said, 'if you need a place to stay tonight, there's a feather bed in that room across the hall and plenty of quilts to keep you warm. You can sleep there.' He thanked me and went to the room. The next morning he was up early, rearin' to help. We fed up, and later, while we was enjoyin' Kate's good breakfast, I told the stranger that I had no money to hire him but if he was down on his luck and wanted to stay with us until he could do better, he was welcome. He was just finishin' off another one of Kate's biscuits, this one drippin' with orange-blossom honey. He wasted no time takin' me up on my offer.

"Ya know, that man didn't have enough fat on his bones to grease a one-egg skillet, but he could put away food like you wouldn't believe. Kate used to smile and say, 'I b'lieve he could eat a horse and chase the rider.' Sometimes, I had to wonder if both of his legs were holler. He shore had a closet somewhere in his skeleton. But, of course, I was gettin' the best end of the bargain, 'cause I wasn't sparin' him from any of the hard jobs. He never balked, and he did the work in a way you couldn't fault him. After some weeks, I began to feel a little shame for workin' this stranger so hard for just his room and board. So one hot day I took him up to the shed, where there was a nice breeze a-blowin' through, and told him I wanted him to sort the potaters. I showed him how he needed to put all the large, perfect potaters in the number one bin; the small, perfect potaters in the number two bin; and all the cut and mis-shaped potaters in the third bin. Then I left to take care of some other things. On my way home for dinner, I stopped by the shed to see how he was gettin' along. Well, I almost dropped my eye-teeth. I found that rascal stretched out on the floor without a dent made in his work.

"'What's wrong?' I asked, figurin' he must be sick.

"'Just plum give out,' he said.

"'What do ya mean, give out? You've spent days out in the sun, splittin' rails, stringin' fence, and diggin' out palmettos, and I give you an easy job in the shade—and in no time you're plum give out? That don't make no sense atall. Somethin' else gotta be wrong.'

"'No, no. You don't understand,' he said, suddenly sittin' up with a potater in each hand. 'It's not the work, mister, but all these decisions. All these decisions, man, done done me under.'

"The next mornin' his room was empty, and I never saw the man again."

I enjoyed Roy's story and, without any prompting on my part, he started another one.

"After Kate was gone," he said, "instead of having more people than I needed out at the farm, I had a hard time gettin' help. One day when I was workin' on my old tractor, a man walked up lookin' for work. I really needed help in the worst way, but when I asked this bozo what he could do, he said, 'I can sleep through a storm.' I crawled out from under my tractor, and asked him again, thinkin' to be sure he ain't heard me right, but again he said, 'I can sleep through a storm.' Well, as bad as I needed help, I weren't in no hurry to get a man who talked like he'd been kicked in the head by a mule. So I told him, 'I don't know, but I may have someone for the job, but if you don't find work, come back Monday.'

"That weekend I tried hard to find some help—even came up here to Jacksonville—but everyone was either workin' for or fightin' in the war. On my way back home, I realized what a mistake I'd made by not rememberin' one of Kate's sayin's, that a bird in hand is worth two in the bush, even if the one in hand is a kook. Sunday night I went to bed prayin' that the man with the weird answer would come back Monday and—you know? —he did! I still felt a little skittish about hirin' him, though. But I soon found out that this feller was all right. He was young and as slow as molasses in January, but I could find no fault with his work. In spite of his pokiness, in three weeks we got the cabbage and potaters gathered.

"That evenin' as I was sittin' on the porch, I saw lightnin' playin' on the horizon. We was havin' a hot, dry spell so I reasoned it was just heat lightnin'. I was tired and I went on to bed. About midnight, thunder woke me up. I got up, pulled on my rubber boots, grabbed my slicker, and rushed to the room across the hall.

"The door was closed. I knocked but got no answer. I knocked again and hollered and tried the door, but it was locked. The storm was bearin' down on us so I rushed out, figurin' I'd at least get the old tractor under kiver and pen up what stock I could.

"I was so agrafretted with a hired man who wouldn't get up when you needed him that I took no notice of the wind and rain, but the lightnin' and thunder was nerve-shatterin'. With every flash of lightnin' and crack of thunder, I swore I'd fire that man before breakfast the next mornin'.

"When I got to the barn, I found that the tractor was already in the shed and had a tarp tied securely over it. The stock was all bedded down, and all the doors and gates was chained. Everything was buckled down. It was rainin' bullfrogs and pitchforks to stack 'em by the time I got back to the house. As I walked down the hall and heard the deep breathin' of the hired man as he slept through the storm, I started re-thinkin' my thinkin'. The man's weird answer started makin' sense. I crawled back in bed and relaxed. As long as I had that man around, I could sleep through a storm too."

A look of peace came over Roy's face. He laid his head back on the pillow and closed his eyes. I tiptoed out of the room. I told my friend about her father's stories. She nodded knowingly. "That last story was about Bill," she said. "We've turned the farm over to him."

Telling time: 12–15 minutes
Audience: middle school–adult

Copy the first two paragraphs of this story and paste them onto a sheet of newsprint. After reading that part, fold the paper, put it down, and finish telling the story. This story can be made into different stories with very little effort. The newspaper article can be told as a one-minute story or combined with either or both of Roy's stories, which can also be told separately.

JumboJim

J im was a big, BIG man, and the scuttlebutt is that after he took his niece to the circus, she started calling him JumboJim instead of Uncle Jim and the name stuck. Of course, there were many who thought it not fitting for a man of his calling. After all, he was, as they say, "a man of the cloth." He had lank, black hair, bronze skin, and chiseled features. Reportedly, his grandmother was a native American, but no one knows from what tribe she came. In fact, it seems no one knows now where JumboJim came from.

One October evening, just as the Florida sun was silhouetting the tall pine and cypress trees against a blaze of color in the western sky, JumboJim rode his gray mare up to Tom's Tavern on the southeast shore of Lake Dorr. He dismounted at the hitching post, brushed the dust from his blue serge suit, smoothed the wrinkles from his coattails, and tucked his Bible under his arm. Standing tall, he walked through the swinging doors.

As one on a mission, he paraded to the bar, put down his Bible, and ordered a cup of sassafras tea. When he turned around, he didn't need to ask for silence for it had followed him through that room like a bloodhound.

A big infectious smile covered his face as he said, "Evenin', folks. My name is Jim Jowers, and I'm your new preacher. I plan to preach my first sermon right here, tonight."

Sitting at one of the tables, two men wearing army uniforms (minus the insignias) started laughing. JumboJim ignored them and continued, "Now, if you'll excuse me, I'll rinse the dust off my vocal cords and then get down to the business of preachin' God's Word."

He then turned, saucered and blew his tea, and started to take a sip when he realized there was something uncanny about the silence. One glance at the reflection in the bar mirror explained the reason: one of

17

the hecklers had a gun pointed in his direction. Keeping a sharp eye on the would-be gunman, he drank his tea, picked up his open Bible with both hands, and slowly turned to face him.

In a calm, confident manner, JumboJim said, "Mister, I don't know what your problem is, but I don't cotton to guns pointed in my direction, so why don't you put yours away?"

"Preacher, don't trouble yoreself 'bout my problems. Looks ter me lak you've got plenty of yore own." A few of the patrons snickered a nervous laugh, and the heckler gained courage. "Now, you jest put that book on the table rat there and step over thar by that pianer. You've showed us that yore head is loose. Let's see iffen yore feet can move as fast as yore tongue. Show us how good you can dance. And, preacher, you'd better do some fast steppin' 'cause good dancers are welcomed here, but preachers need to take their business elsewhere." The raucous crowd laughed and applauded the spokesman.

JumboJim put his open Bible on the table, straightened up to his full height and said, "That was not a part of the program I planned for tonight, but if that is the order of the day, I'll do my best to fit in."

He paused, quickly sized up the situation, and then said, "I always perform best when I ask my Lord for His blessing before I begin. I do want to do my best, so let's all reverently bow our heads, and I'll word my prayer and then get on with the business at hand."

The hellion was a little unnerved by the cool action of this big stranger, but he was really distracted when, one after another, the patrons bowed their heads as JumboJim got to his knees and started praying.

"My Dear Lord, God and ruler over all things, how great Thou art! Yet You commissioned me, a mere speck in Your Universe, to preach Your word. Lord, in humble obedience, I am here to do that. I do not ask that You remove the thorns, pitfalls, or even the boulders in my path. I only ask that You, Lord, will see fit to give me the wisdom, strength, and tools so that I, with Your blessing, can take care of the problems myself. Amen."

JumboJim was back on his feet in a blink of an eye, and when the patrons looked up, they were shocked to see the tall man holding not one but two six-shooters with the dexterity of a professional gunman. His draw from under his coat was so fast and smooth that many were convinced that God had miraculously placed those guns in his hands.

His commanding voice filled the room as he said, "Mister, I don't like gun play and only use it when I'm forced to, but don't expect me to tell you the second time so listen carefully. Turn your gun around and lay it right there beside my Bible and do it now."

Without any hesitation, the troublemaker did as he was told.

Still holding his guns, JumboJim said, "Now, either I speak or these do!" His message was loud and clear. The patrons were filled with awe. Quickly, a reverent atmosphere prevailed, and the folks were in a receptive mood for his sermon. JumboJim put his guns down, picked up his Bible, read Dr. Luke's account of Jesus teaching His followers to love their enemies, and then JumboJim preached a powerful sermon on the golden rule. He finished his sermon and stood there letting his closing words sink in. Then he smiled and said, "Now, if there is anyone here who can play that piano, I know the words to 'Amazing Grace'."

Sometime during the singing, the heckler and his buddy slipped out. When JumboJim pronounced the benediction, a sharp dresser approached him, gave his name, extended his hand, and said, "I am with the Kismet Land and Improvement Company. As you may or may not know, we have just opened a fifty-room luxury hotel on the square in Kismet. I came to Florida planning to spend the winter, but an emergency has necessitated my going back home. I liked the way you handled the precarious situation tonight and am willing to offer you the use of my suite, your meals at the hotel dining room, and a small stipend in exchange for your service as general manager until I can return. You will be in a position to meet people, and you will have plenty of time to preach as I have good dependable help."

JumboJim smiled and said, "The Lord does work in wondrous ways. If you have a vacancy tonight and a stable for my horse, I'll walk over with you and talk about it."

Thus, JumboJim became the general manager of Kismet's crown jewel, the minister of the gospel, a goodwill ambassador, keeper of the peace, and the construction overseer of a church building. His integrity, enthusiasm, and sense of humor made him a popular legend while he was still residing in the growing community. Folks liked to tease and talk about him. They especially liked to tell about his first sermon in Tom's Tavern and his first baptisms in Lake Dorr. He had just finished administering the rite to the last candidate when a large alligator chased the big man out of the lake.

Like fish tales, gator tales get better with the telling. One day when Hiram, the acknowledged ace of store-porch storytellers, was demonstrating his mastery of the art to a larger-than-usual audience, a newcomer challenged Hiram's description of how fast JumboJim got out of the lake.

"You don't really expect me to believe that this man walked on water?" asked the doubting tourist.

The old codger removed his hat and scratched his head. After thinking about it for a minute, Hiram said, "Wall, I wouldn't want you or anyone ter go away sayin' that I said that JumboJim *walked* on water. 'Cause when he came outten of that lake, he was movin' so fast that even the big man couldn't a been walkin'—he'd had ta been *runnin'* on water."

Many Florida Crackers will tell you that the Big Freeze of 1889 killed every citrus fruit tree in the two-year-old county of Lake and that people by the score packed up and left, looking for greener pastures. Whether or not you believe that to be the gospel truth, history will bear out that, soon after the big freeze, Kismet rolled up its sidewalks, took in the doorsteps, and took its place on the list of Florida's ghost towns. The fifty-room hotel was dismantled and reassembled on the southeast corner of the intersection of Magnolia Avenue and Grove Street in downtown Eustis. It served Eustis residents and visitors as the Grand View Hotel for many years. Around 1955, it was torn down and a bank building built on the site.

And what happened to JumboJim? The last word I had on him, he was sitting tall in his saddle as he rode his gray mare off into the sunset.

Telling time: 10–12 minutes

Audience: Because of this story's subtle humor, which is not understood or appreciated by most children, adults are the best audience for this story.

Mastodon Hunt

In the 1800s there were still numerous fossil remains on the surface of the ground throughout the center of the state. Most of them were easy to identify, but the mastodon bones, retrieved from at least two different springs in Florida, gave everyone's imagination room to speculate, for no one then living had ever seen this colossal animal. From the bones, a person could get an idea of its size, and thoughtful people figured if his voice was proportionate to his body, he must have made the earth tremble, not only with his body weight but also with his voice vibrations. When they considered how much food an animal of that size would devour, they were truly thankful that it no longer stalked their homeland. At least, they hoped none of them were still lurking around, but much of Florida was still unexplored.

It was when commercial passenger boats first navigated the Ocklawaha River that, early one morning, the inhabitants of the Ocali Forests were aroused from their slumbers by a loud, strange noise. An old hunter named Matt Driggers, whose ear was trained to discern the scream of the panther, the howl of the wolf, or the growl of the bear, rushed out, exclaiming, "What on airth is that?"

The sound was heard again and Matt grabbed his hunting horn and blew a blast that brought his faithful hounds whining at his feet. After taking his rifle, Dead Shot, from its hooks, he saddled and mounted his horse and took off at a gallop. He soon arrived at the home of his nearest neighbor, Pat Kennedy.

"Hullow, Pat! Ere you in thar asleep? How can ya be when the devil hisself is unchained outten in this here swamp? Didn't ya hear 'im?"

"Oh, Matt, that's nothin' but one of 'em old masterdons!" Pat said as he sauntered out onto his porch with his rifle cradled in his arm. "Ya know we dun seed his bones where he was drowned in the spring."

"I dunno. Maybe so," Matt said thoughtfully while he scratched his head. "But one thing's sartin: he's a mighty big varmint an' his voice is curoser than anything I ever heard afore in my time."

Pat thought about the situation a minute or two and then said, "Well, one thing for sartin: there's nothin' rangin' these here parts that my dogs and Kill Quick here can't bring 'im down." He stroked his rifle and called all his dogs, and he and Matt were soon on their way to the house of the next frontiersman.

The baying of hounds and the blowing of horns created an excitement that ran like wildfire throughout the woods until all the settlers were collected. After reviewing his comrades and counting the dogs, Matt Driggers was satisfied that the full force of the country was mustered. He took the lead, riding bravely through bushes and swamps, fording creeks, and swimming lagoons in pursuit of the great "varmint." When he figured that they were close enough, he gave orders to put the dogs on the trail. Each man called his dogs, but as they were coaxing the dogs to pick up the trail, the huge monster trumpeted again. The echo not only sent the dogs cowering back to their masters, but the masters back to their mounts. The horses stood frozen in their tracks.

Matt, bolder than the rest, regained his courage. Leading his horse, he stepped forward and said, "Come on, boys. If the dogs are scared, we'll follow the sound!"

With much misgivings, they cautiously followed Matt in the direction of the sound until they reached the basin of Silver Springs. There they found a number of strangers and a strange-looking boat being unloaded. The hunters started questioning the people who were milling around about the great monster. When the folks seemed ignorant of what they were talking about, the hunters tried to imitate the sounds they had heard. After much bedlam, the captain asked Matt to quiet the hunters. He then stepped up on a wooden box on the deck and said, "I think I know what you are so excited about, and I am glad to tell you that you need to have no fear, for you are standing on the deck of the monster. What you heard was only a steamboat whistle." But, having never heard one, they were not convinced that he spoke the truth. In defense of his honor, the captain built up a good head of steam, opened the throttle, and let them hear, at close proximity, the steam whistle.

The whistle startled them and they jumped (as some of you just did), but soon they were laughing and they laughed all the way home.

Telling time: 8–10 minutes
Audience: 4th grade–adult

Since some of today's audiences may not be familiar with the sound of a steam whistle, a good reproduction of the sound makes a great finale to this story.

Marooning on the Matanzas

I
t was 1880, and the War Between the States was an ordeal of the past. The South, while not restored to its former splendor, offered many business opportunities to young men. Len, Frank, and Dell, diplomas in hand, stood outside the Bishop Business Institute, rehashing their plans to go south.

Frank and Dell soon shared an office overlooking the riverfront at the cotton exchange, and Len found his niche with the Rice Growers Co-op in the busy town of Savannah. As the season offered the men leisure, they spent the time exploring their latest fascination, Southern culture.

"You know, I really like those grits they eat every morning for breakfast," Dell said. "But I'm sure, with just a little effort, a more savory name could be given to the dish."

Frank agreed and added, "There's nothing more distasteful to me than grit in my food. But have you noticed the expression these Southerners use for a camping trip?"

"Yes, but 'marooned' suggests adventure, and I like it." There was silence for a few minutes as both men stared at the sweltering mist rising from the river. Then Dell suddenly exclaimed, "I've a capital idea! Let's go marooning! Business is slow and it's too hot to work, so let's find Len and the three of us go marooning on the Matanzas."

"Why the Matanzas? That is south of San Augustin."

"I've heard that the Tybee and other marooning spots around here are so crowded that it is hard to find a spot to pitch your tent."

"Then Matanzas it is!"

Before the sun was up the next morning, Dell, Frank, and Len loaded their camping equipment and supplies on the *Florida Cannonball Express* and climbed aboard. After eight hours of whirling through fragrant pine forests and whitening cotton fields, they arrived at the gates of San Augustin.

Covered with dust and cinders but full of enthusiastic anticipation, the three men trudged up the narrow shell road while the sun was still beating down in a glare of white heat. When they reached the hotel Sea View, they not only rented a room for the night but arranged with their host for a ten-day lease of his new cat boat, the *Eloise*.

The natty little craft was soon hauled alongside the hotel landing stairs and the camp supplies stowed away under the half deck. When the supper bell sounded, they had everything in readiness to take advantage of the early morning tide. After supper they strolled up the broad sea-walk to old Fort San Marcos, where young Minorcans were dancing. Before returning to the Sea View, they filled their water containers at the Fountain of Youth.

The next morning they were awakened by the porter's soft knock and voice saying, "Daylight, sah!" As the *Eloise* made her way to meet the sunrise, the only living thing her occupants could see was a sleepy look-ing sentinel pacing up and down in front of the old U.S. barracks.

As the city sank from view behind the salt marshes, the wind fresh-ened, and the *Eloise* soon was moving swimmingly along a straight stretch of the Matanzas River. The kettle, under Len's skillful manipula-tion, sang merrily on the little oil stove, and they enjoyed coffee, hot and strong, with chicken sandwiches.

Soon, white sand dunes appeared on the port side, and the hoarse roaring of the surf was heard on the wind. They passed the remains of old Fort Matanzas and glided out in full view of the ocean, but they stayed close-reefed across the inlet and came to anchor in the mouth of a deep creek. They decided to pitch camp on the south bank.

They pitched a nine-by-nine wall tent to sleep in and a small tent-fly to shelter the cook from sun and rain on the hard sand just above the high-water mark. They happily donned their marooning togs, which consisted of palmetto sombreros, sleeveless cotton knit shirts, and light-weight denim overalls. Dell and Frank went in search of a well that was marked on a rough chart that Dell had picked up in San Augustin. When they returned, they found Len cleaning his morning catch. So for din-ner they had fried mullet, roasted sweet potatoes, corn dodgers, and indi-gestion.

A strong onshore wind blew away their plans to spend the after-noon surf fishing. They rolled their overalls up to their knees and ran barefoot races up and down the shore, slid and rolled down the steep sand dunes, and pushed each other into the combing surf. All this horse-play by three dignified businessmen, whose aggregate age exceeded seven decades, might have convinced even a skeptic that there were magical properties in the water from the Fountain of Youth. Before the afternoon was spent, the indigestion was forgotten and the evening meal was welcomed.

Seated around the mush pot that evening, they planned a seven-day program of sports that sounded like a chapter from *Robinson Crusoe*. The wind departed with the sun, and a host of mosquitoes swooped down on the camp, driving the campers under the mosquito bar. There they lay awake for hours, listening to the skipping and flopping of the small fry in the shallows.

About midnight, a school of riotous porpoises sailed up the creek to a point opposite the camp. There they proceeded to have a party! Grunting and snorting like a drove of wild hogs, they bumped into the *Eloise* and churned the water into foam around her. They ran the alligators ashore, picked quarrels with the sharks, and finally got into a free-for-all running fight among themselves that carried them out into the deep water.

As the sun peeped over the peaceful ocean, the three campers were snoozing like healthy infants, and a clear soprano voice fell upon the drowsy stillness, singing an old song of the sea.

> Oh! A long, long pull, and a strong, strong pull;
> Cheerily, my lads, heave-ho!

The "lads" were awake in an instant.

"Mermaids," said Frank, pulling on his overalls.

"Sirens!" cried Len, who had glued his right eye to a little peephole in the tent door.

In a desperate struggle for first place at the peephole, Frank and Dell tumbled over Len and landed outside the tent. They sat up just in time to see a white skiff glide into the mouth of the creek, with a pretty young lady in the bow. In the stern, a fine-looking old gentleman, dressed in white, held a large sun umbrella over a dignified lady in black. In the rower's seat, two pretty girls smiled and rested on their oars as the boat swung around broadside to the shore.

"I trust," said the gentleman with a gracious wave of his hand, "that you will pardon this intrusion." Then he went on to explain that they had been camping at Moultrie Creek during the past week and had just dropped down with the ebb tide on the way to their last summer's camping ground, located about four miles up the creek. They had hoped to reach their destination in time for a late breakfast but found the current so strong that they must wait for the tide to turn.

Frank, with a rueful glance at his sunburned, sprawling feet, walked to the water's edge and stammered something about being most happy. As the old gentleman stepped ashore, he introduced himself as Mr. Perkins of Montgomery, Alabama, and the ladies as his wife and daughters.

The flood tide rippled around the prow of the *Eloise,* the kettle of dishwater boiled itself dry, and the fire went out while they chatted over their empty coffee cups. At last, Mr. Perkins, consulting his watch and a tide table, announced that the hour for departure had arrived. He arose and extended to his hosts a cordial invitation to visit him in camp and in city.

As the skiff drifted away from the shore, a sleepy-looking, young black man thrust his head over the gunwale of a little baggage punt that the skiff was towing. He gazed back wistfully toward a plateful of fried mush, the surface of which the sun had baked to the consistency of a firebrick.

Dell grabbed the plate, dumped its contents into an old newspaper, rolled the paper into a ball, and threw it with all his might toward the boy. The missile passed high over the intended receiver. It hit the back of Mr. Perkins' head, knocked off his hat, burst open and scattered fried mush in every direction.

The ladies screamed in chorus. As for Mr. Perkins, he simply passed his handkerchief across the back of his head, replaced his hat in the most deliberate manner, and, opening the big umbrella, brought it around so as to hide the occupants of the boat from view. The former hosts could only stand and gaze helplessly at the receding umbrella. At last Dell found his tongue and, as usual in such a crisis, succeeded in making himself misunderstood.

"Sir!" he cried. "Believe me, I did not mean to hit you!"

Slowly the big umbrella went up, until Mr. Perkins' striking countenance came into view. As he shot an indignant glance backward, he said, with impressive dignity. "So you were only trying to see how close you could come to me without hitting me, eh? Gentlemen, when you have framed a suitable apology for this outrage, you will find me willing to take its acceptance under consideration. Again I wish you good day."

Then the big umbrella dropped into place, like the falling of the curtain on the last act of a doleful tragedy. The polished oars flashed swiftly in the sunlight and the white skiff was soon out of sight beyond a sharp bend of the creek.

"What are we going to do about it?" Frank asked, as the boat disappeared.

"Do? Why, we are going to cut across the bend, head them off, and demand an immediate audience! That's what we are going to do," Dell said.

Hastily, they pulled on their knee boots and struck out across country, with Dell in the lead. They trudged through swamps where the mud was knee-deep and water moccasins were plentiful, cut their way through a tangle of scrub oaks and wild grapevines, and struggled through clumps of palmettos. They arrived at the creek just in time to hear a sweet, coaxing voice say, "Now, dear Papa, please don't scold us for laughing, for we really can't help it."

When the boat came into view they could see Mamma Perkins drying her eyes with a pretty handkerchief, and still she laughed. Papa Perkins was now failing miserably in his efforts to look stern and dignified. Suddenly the old gentleman leaned back in his seat and joined heartily in the laughter.

The young black man sat up in the punt and regarded Mr. Perkins apprehensively. "Say, Mars Perkin! All de time, I spec' dat 'ere passel of frie' mush was tended fo' me 'cause dat man, he look so at me w'en he frowed hit."

"Now or never!" Dell said, as Mr. Perkins again burst out with laughter.

The three bedraggled men stepped out onto the narrow margin of sand just as the skiff came opposite them.

Dell started in at once, "Mr. Perkins, allow me to detain you while I explain this unfortunate affair."

"Glad to see you, gentlemen. Glad to see you, indeed!" Mr. Perkins cordially extended his hand as the boat was laid alongside. "Explanations are quite unnecessary—quite! I see it all plainly now. It is all right, sirs, all right. Again, we will bid you good day, for the tide slackens. Remember, we desire your further acquaintances."

Once more the sun was shining, the fish jumping, and the birds singing. The marooners followed the creek back to their campsite. As they went, they skimmed sand dollars across the water and made the old woods ring with shouts of youthful laughter.

Telling time: 15–18 minutes
Audience: middle school–adult

The length of this story and its cast of characters make it a difficult one to tell to children, even though they do enjoy this type of humor. An older male teller might shorten the story by telling it in first person (as Dell) and make an audience of fourth graders listen spellbound. Remember, much of the appeal of this story is its timeframe. Don't cut the historical nuggets.

The Indian Legend of Silver Springs in Florida

A long time ago, when Okahumkee was king over the tribes of Indians who roamed and hunted around the Southwestern lakes, an event occurred which filled many hearts with sorrow. The king had a daughter named Weenonah, whose rare beauty was the pride of the old man's life. Weenonah was exceedingly graceful and symmetrical in figure. Her face was of an olive complexion, tinged with light brown, her skin finely transparent, exquisitely clear. It was easy to see the red blood beneath the surface, and often it blushed in response to the impulses of a warm and generous nature. Her eye was the crystal of the soul—clear and liquid, or flashing and defiant, according to her mood. But the hair was the glory of the woman. Dark as the raven's plume, but shot with gleams of sacred arrows, the large masses, when free, rolled in tresses of rich abundance. The silken drapery of that splendid hair fell about her 'like some royal cloak dropped from the cloud-land's rare and radiant loom.' Weenonah was, in truth, a forest-belle—an idol of the braves—and many were the eloquent things said of her by the red men, when they rested at noon, or smoked around the evening fires. She was a coveted prize, while chiefs and warriors vied with each other as to who should present the most valuable gift when her hand was sought from the king, her father. But the daughter had already seen and loved Chuleotah, the renowned chief of a tribe which dwelt among the wild groves near Silver Springs.

The personal appearance of Chuleotah, as described by the hieroglyphics of that day, could be no other than prepossessing. He was arrayed in a style suitable to the dignity of a chief. Bold, handsome, well-developed, he was to an Indian maiden the very ideal of manly vigor. But it was a sad truth that between the old chief and the young, and their tribes, there had long been a deadly feud. They were enemies. When Okahumkee learned that Chuleotah had gained the affections of his beloved child, he at once declared his purpose of revenge. A war of passion was soon opened and carried on without much regard to international amenities; nor had many weeks passed away before the noble Chuleotah was slain—slain, too, by the father of Weenonah.

Dead! Her lover dead! Poor Weenonah! Will she return to the paternal lodge, and dwell among her people, while her father's hand is stained with the drippings of her lover's scalp? No; she hurries away to the well-known fountain. Her heart is there; for it is a favorite spot, and was a trysting-place, where she and Chuleotah met. Its associations are all made sacred by the memories of the past, while on the glassy bosom of the spring the pale ghost of Chuleotah stands beckoning her to come. 'Yes, my own, my beloved one, I come. I will follow where thou leadest, to the green and flowery land.' Thus spake the will, if not the lips, of the maiden. It is not a mere common suicide which she now contemplates; it is not because she is sick of the world, or tired of life. Her faith is, that by an act of self-immolation she will join her lover on that spirit-plain, whose far-off, strange glory has now for her such an irresistible attraction.

The red clouds of sunset had passed away from the western skies. Gray mists came stealing on, but they soon melted and disappeared, as the stars shone through the airy blue. The moon came out with more than common brilliancy, and her light silvered the fountain. All was still, save the night-winds, that sighed and moaned through the lofty pines.

Then came Weenonah to the side of the spring, where, gazing down, she could see on the bottom the clear, green shelves of limestone, sloping into sharp hollows, opening here and there into still profounder depths. Forty feet below, on the mass of rock, was her bed of death—easy enough for her, as before she could reach it the spirit must have fled. The jagged rocks on the floor could therefore produce no pain in that beautiful form. For a moment she paused on the edge of the spring, then met her palms above her head, and with a wild leap she fell into the whelming waves.

Down there in the spring are shells, finely polished by the attrition of the waters. They shine with purple and crimson, mingled with white irradiations, as if beams of the Aurora, or clouds of a tropical sunset, had been broken and scattered among them. Now, mark those long, green filaments of moss, or fresh-water algae, swaying to and fro to the motion of the waves; these are the loosened braids of Weenonah's hair, whose coronet gives us such beautiful coruscations, sparkling and luminous, like diamonds of the deep, when in the phosphorescence of night the ocean waves are tipped with fire. These relics of the devoted Indian girl are the charm of Silver Springs. But as to Weenonah herself—the real woman who could think and feel, with her affections and memory—she has gone to one of those enchanted isles far out in the western sea, where the maiden and her lover are united, and where both have found another Silver Spring, amid the rosy bowers of love eternal.

Telling time: 8–9 minutes
Audience: 4th grade–adult

This legend, taken from Petals Plucked from Sunny Climes, *published in 1880, seems so much in keeping with what might have been reality, we have copied it for the benefit of those who are fond of legendary tales.*

The Legend of Bernice and Claire

About one hundred years ago, among the settlers in the vicinity of Fort King, lived a proud and haughty Carolinian, Captain Harding Douglass. His only son, Claire, fell in love with Bernice Mayo.

Bernice's father had sold his homeplace in Virginia and moved his wife to Florida, hoping her health would improve. They settled near the Oklawaha River, where Bernice was born. When Bernice was eight years old, her mother got "swamp fever" and died. Three years later Bernice and her father moved to Silver Springs. He had spent all his savings and hired out as a lumberjack. Bernice was left alone from before daylight until after dark, with only Aunt Silla, an old black woman, to keep an eye on her. Although Bernice had neither the clothes nor ornaments to enhance her appearance, she was soon turning heads everywhere she went. Her thin body moved with grace. Her blonde hair was her golden crown. Her eyes were the color of—and her features were as delicate and perfect as—a violet.

Bernice and Claire met when Claire came to Silver Springs, which he often did. From the first time he met Bernice, he was infatuated with her and, from their first meeting, found ways for them to spend time together in and around beautiful Silver Springs. At last, Claire declared his love for her and gave her a gold chain bracelet. She was hesitant to accept the gift, but when he apologized for it not being something better, she accepted it.

"Here," Claire said, "let me fasten it around your wrist to symbolize how my love will forever surround you."

Bernice was so excited! She had long loved Claire, but she knew that her father was right—that she shouldn't get her heart set on him. She now trembled with excitement as she waited to share her happiness with her father. He took a good look at the bracelet and said, "Looks like real gold, but, Berny-Baby, I wouldn't get my heart set on marryin' him, no matter what he says, for I don't believe the Captain will let it ever happen."

Her father's reaction caused a cloud to pass over Bernice's sun, but a few miles away Claire's sun was in total eclipse. Young Douglass boldly faced his father and declared his love for and determination to marry Bernice Mayo. A terrible scene followed. The proud Captain swore, "Why, I'd rather see you dead than married to that Mayo tramp."

When the Captain found that nothing he said could sway his son, he tried a different approach. He said, "Son, I'm glad to see that you've got the diplomacy and courage of a mature man. I was undecided, but now I'm convinced that you can handle my pending business deal in England. Go and take care of it, and when you get back, you shall have your wedding with my blessing."

Claire, flabbergasted by this long-desired stamp of approval and painfully aware that he could make life easier for Bernice if his father approved of the marriage, agreed to go. The hurried note that he wrote for Bernice and asked one of the servants to deliver was intercepted by the Captain, as were all of Claire's letters to Bernice. It was a month before Bernice learned what had happened. Then she lived for the day when she would receive a letter from Claire assuring her of his unfailing love and giving her hope that he would return.

A year dragged slowly by with no word from Claire. Broken-hearted and filled with despair, Bernice slowly wasted away, daily becoming more and more fragile, until, little more than a ghost of her former self, she half staggered, half crept to Silver Springs and fell fainting into the arms of Aunt Silla. Recovering consciousness, the dying girl begged the kindly old woman to grant her last request.

"I have come here to die," she said. "Tonight, when the moon rises, row my body to the Boiling Springs and bury me beneath the waters."

Aunt Silla did not want Bernice to die, so she pleaded with her not to give up, all in vain. Filled with superstitious fear at carrying out such an eerie mission, she argued that she couldn't do it. Suddenly Bernice raised her wasted body and gazed with unnaturally bright eyes into the face of Aunt Silla.

"I am a dying woman," she gasped. "I have talked with God and He has answered me. Though my love has been taken from me in life, it shall not be so in death. Within twenty-four hours from the time my body lies at the bottom of Boiling Springs, Claire shall join me there. If you fail to carry out my dying wishes, evil will befall you and you will ever be haunted by my dying curse."

With chattering teeth and rolling eyes, Aunt Silla promised, and with a contented smile upon her waxen face, Bernice Mayo sank back in death. When the moon spread its soft glow over the waters, Aunt Silla carried the body of the girl to the shore of the pool, placed her tenderly in a small boat, and rowed silently to the spot where, far beneath the surface, the water boiled and bubbled from a great mysterious crack in the rocky bottom of the pool. Lifting the dead girl and muttering a prayer, she placed the body on the calm water, and, with tears streaming down her black cheeks, watched it sink slowly into the depths.

Then suddenly, as if by some miracle, the bubbling, seething springs ceased, and as the mortal remains of Bernice Mayo reached the crack and disappeared, the rocks slowly closed above the body. Filled with terror at the supernatural scene she had witnessed, Aunt Silla rowed hastily ashore, ran to her hut, fell to her knees and prayed until morning. When the sunshine was gleaming brilliantly on the waters of the pool and the events of the night seemed more like a dream than a reality, she got to her feet, washed her face, and prepared and ate breakfast. Now, her curiosity was overcoming her dread. She walked down to the water's edge and, shoving the boat from shore, paddled toward the spot where Bernice had vanished.

Unknown to Aunt Silla, Claire Douglass had returned to his father's home during the night. There he had met his richly adorned cousin, whom his father had selected as his son's future bride.

"How would you young people like to take a row on Silver Springs?" he asked at the breakfast table. "I have a new boat, and if you do not object I'll join you."

At the mention of the spot where he and Bernice had spent so many happy hours, an overwhelming desire to see her swept over young Douglass, and he gladly agreed. As the party reached the shores of the pool and embarked on the boat, they noticed another boat resting motionless near the Boiling Springs, its only occupant Aunt Silla, who ignored their presence and continued to peer into the depths with tear-filled eyes.

As the Douglass boat reached the spot and the three gazed into the crystal water, the cousin suddenly cried out, "Oh, see, there is something that looks like a hand—a human hand!"

Staring but not believing what they saw, the two men watched the boiling waters die down to reveal a white hand and arm with a golden chain locked about the wrist. Instantly young Douglass recognized it. His face paled, and dread and fear clutched at his heart. And then his amazement increased when the rocks seemed to part and he saw the body of his loved one resting on the bottom of the pool, a smile upon her face, her golden hair surrounding her head like a halo.

With a wild, heart-piercing cry, the young man plunged into the pool, diving straight downward toward the form of the girl whose life had been sacrificed to love. Speechless with awe, his father and his cousin watched as Claire swam deeper and deeper into the mysterious cavern, until, reaching the body of Bernice, he seized her in his arms. And then, before their staring eyes, the rocky walls drew together, and from the spot where the lovers had vanished the water boiled and bubbled and hid everything from view.

Today, visitors to Silver Springs may gaze downward at the Bridal Chamber, where the waters seethe upward from the crack eighty feet beneath the surface, bringing with it a constant stream of tiny, pearly shells. And on the rocky bottom, you may see curious plants with lily-like leaves and waxen, white flowers known as the Bernice Bridal Wreath. Among the young people of the area, these strange underwater blossoms are highly prized, for there is a local belief that any maiden who receives one of the blooms as a gift will be a happy bride within the year.

Aunt Silla, who lived well into the twentieth century, related this story and told of the part she played in the drama many times. As late as the 1930s, many of the old residents of the area around Silver Springs vouched for the unvarnished truth of the legend of Claire Douglass and Bernice Mayo.

Telling time: 10–12 minutes
Audience: 5th grade–adult

Whirlwind

A delbert, or Dell, as everyone called him, hobbled as fast as he could to help his father fold the sheep, for the clouds that suddenly covered the sun portended a bad storm. A jagged bolt of lightning flashed through the atmosphere. A deafening crash of thunder followed. Several small whirlwinds danced through the corral, picking up debris in their paths. A high-spirited stallion, spooked by the commotion, snorted, jumped the rail fence, and raced wildly toward the nearby scrub. The mares followed, and a young colt tried to jump the fence but caught his leg in the rails and fell.

"Dell," his father called, "go as quickly as you can, son, to the big house and tell Squire Jowers what's happened."

Dell, crippled since birth, wanted to comfort the colt, but he did as his father told him. Rain, mingled with hailstones, pelted him as he hurried on as fast as he could.

Squire Jowers looked at the crippled boy, standing at his door with water dripping into puddles around his feet (which always seemed to be going in opposite directions). Realizing the effort Dell had put forth, Squire Jowers was filled with empathy. He thanked Dell and assured him that he himself would come see about the colt. Then he called to his foreman to get some men to round up the runaways.

The rain stopped as suddenly as it started. Dell hobbled back to the paddock. The colt lay in a mud puddle, his nostrils quivering and his muscles twitching. Reassuring the colt in a low voice, Dell slowly approached him. The colt made a feeble effort to get to his feet but, snorting with pain, lay back down.

"There, boy. There, boy, take it easy. I'm not going to hurt you." Dell sat in the mud, pillowed the colt's head on his knee and stroked its neck.

Dell's father got the sheep secured and quieted. He arrived at the corral about the same time as did Squire. Gently, they examined the colt as Dell continued to stroke and reassure it.

With bitter disappointment evident in his voice, Squire concluded, "His leg is definitely broken, he has two nasty gashes in his sides, and he is badly bruised. He may have internal injuries as well. You might as well get him out of his misery."

"No. No," cried out Dell. "Please . . . please don't kill him. I'll care for him. Please, kind sir, let me. I'll bind his leg and anoint his bruises, feed and care for him till he's able to walk again."

"Son," said his father, "you don't understand. He will probably never walk again, and if he does, he'll always limp."

"But, Papa, please let me try to make him well. Limping is not all that bad!"

Squire looked at Dell's twisted legs and, in a voice that broke with pent-up feelings, said to Dell's father, "I'll leave the decision to you. Do what you think best."

"Please, Papa, help me get him home. Mama will make a sling for him, and you can set his leg like you did that ewe's. I'll take care of him. You won't have to turn your hand."

Against his better judgment, Dell's father and two other farm hands got the colt on a sled and took it to the small combination-barn-and-stable in back of the four-room house in which Dell and his parents lived.

"I guess I should not have given in to him," he said to his wife. "But he pleaded so hard. I'm afraid caring for the colt will place a needless burden on you. The colt will probably suffer and eventually die. Letting the boy get more attached to it will just make the medicine more bitter for him to swallow, and he surely has had his share of it already."

"I understand your concern, but I'm glad that you gave in. It will be good for the boy to care for the colt, and if it dies, he will have to learn to accept that too," Dell's mother said as she finished securing the braided strips to the old mattress ticking that she had made into front and back slings.

When the colt was supported with the slings, his wounds and bruises treated and his broken leg carefully splinted and bound, he seemed to be comfortable.

"Thank you, Papa," Dell said. "I'm so glad that you didn't kill this beautiful colt. See how he's breathing easy. He's going to live and run again. You'll see. What's his name?"

"Son, I don't know that Squire had named him. He was especially proud of this colt and wanted a name to suit his personality."

"I'm going to call him Whirlwind. That'll always be my name for him," Dell said as he made a pallet of old quilts and corn shucks.

Dell slept in the corn crib, close to Whirlwind, every night for weeks. Whirlwind continued to heal, and, when the binding was taken from the broken leg, it was evident that the set had been good, for it was healing straight.

"Son," said his father as he rewrapped the injured leg, "you must be careful now that he doesn't rebreak it."

Dell was ever so careful. He walked the horse slowly about each day, gently massaged the lame leg, and put him back into the slings each night. At last Whirlwind was taken to the pasture, where his recovery hastened. Dell's parents were still fearful and kept reminding him not to get his hopes up too much. It was not until all the swelling was gone from the lame leg and Whirlwind was cavorting around the pasture that they allowed themselves to bask in the delight of victory.

One day as Dell watched Whirlwind running around the pasture, he fell to wondering if Whirlwind would let him ride on his back. When Whirlwind came up to eat his favorite clover, which Dell gathered each day for him, Dell led him to the silo steps and scampered onto his back. Dell's mother looked up from her work and saw what Dell was doing. She started to cry out a warning, but it was too late. She choked the scream—it would only excite the colt and increase her son's chances of being hurt. To her surprise, Whirlwind walked around as if he knew what precious cargo he had on his back.

Dell's spirits soared.

When Dell's father saw him on Whirlwind's back, he knew that it was time to return the colt to its rightful owner. Joyful pride was damp-ened with tears as Dell rode Whirlwind up to the big house. He would see him again, he was sure, but it wouldn't be the same. He wiped his eyes and nose on his shirtsleeve and knocked on the door.

"Squire, sir, I have come to return your colt."

Again, Squire Jowers looked at the crippled boy standing at his door, and then he saw the beautiful sorrel colt at the hitching post. He was speechless. He walked out and examined the colt's leg, looked at his sleek coat and classical features, stroked the beautiful mane. Then, he trotted him around in a circle.

"He is every bit the horse that I imagined he would be," Squire finally said. "Yes, this one would improve anyone's herd." It was evident that Squire was troubled by his thoughts. Suddenly he said, "But the horse is not mine, son. He's yours, and I cannot be so thieving as to take him from you."

Now the tears did flow. Dell was so excited that he failed to thank Squire. He only cried for joy and repeated over and over, "Whirlwind, you are mine! You are mine!" He hurried back to share the good news with his parents. His mother wiped her eyes with the corner of her apron and gave Dell a big hug. But his father said, "If the horse is yours, we can no longer feed him from Squire's silos."

"Don't worry, Papa," said Dell. "Tomorrow I'll find a way to earn his feed." And he did. On Whirlwind's back, he was able to go from farm to farm and perform odd jobs—shelling corn, peas, and peanuts for planting; weeding gardens; and watching young children while mothers helped their husbands in the fields. Anything he could do, he did in exchange for corn, oats, or millet for Whirlwind.

Each day as Dell returned home, he gave Whirlwind the reins, and day after day he ran faster and faster. Soon he ran with the speed of his namesake. Dell was no longer the little crippled boy whom people pitied but the proud owner of Whirlwind, the fastest and finest horse in all of Marion County.

Telling time: 12–15 minutes
Audience: 3rd grade–adult

Florida ranks second only to Kentucky in the breeding of racehorses. Marion County alone has six hundred horse farms ranging in size from ten acres to five thousand acres. While this story is set in Marion County, the incidents took place before the days of farm specialization, that is, before farms specialized in only one product, e.g., horses, cotton, etc.

Although this is rather a long story for third graders, I have found that children quickly identify with another child and usually have empathy for a crippled one. I have told "Whirlwind" when every child in the audience seemed spellbound—still and quiet for several moments after I finished.

Introduction
Historical Stories

The five historical stories presented here are about three colorful characters. Known by their nicknames—Pogy, Fingy, and Peggy—these movers and shakers left their mark on the Sunshine State.

Pogy Bill was sheriff of Okeechobee County for fourteen years. He had no children of his own, but he was the unofficial daddy of every orphan in the county and a role model for every boy who knew him.

Fingy Conners was a "corned-beef-and-cabbage" man who wintered among the high-society gents and dames of Palm Beach. The road he financed from Florida's east coast to Okeechobee brought Ford's tin-lizzies to the Everglades.

The attractive, witty, and vivacious Margaret (Peggy) O'Neale Eaton was Florida's First Lady from 1834 to 1836. She was also, according to Gene Burnett in Volume 1 of *Florida's Past*, "the object of gossip so scandalous that it caused a vice president to fall, a dark horse to succeed him, a national party to split, and an entire cabinet to resign."

Do Tell!

William E. Collins

I t seems that his name was William, but the "fellers" called him Bill—Pogy Bill. And the "fellers" included bank presidents and bean pickers and all those in between. William E. Collins was born of American parents on the twenty-fourth day of May 1884. His birth took place on an American vessel, which at the time was anchored in the harbor of Sydney, Australia. A child of the sea, Bill took on many of her attributes—wild and strong, with magnetism and grit.

Not much is known concerning his early life. He spent some of his teen years working on cargo ships. Tiring of this strenuous existence, he jumped ship at Buenos Aires and made his way across the Andes to Chile's Pacific coast and from there to Florida. Somewhere along the way, he served a stint in the U.S. Navy. It was there that he was taught the sport of boxing.

He cleared land in central Florida before taking a job as a boiler-maker in Tampa. Here, he became embroiled in some local politics. His convictions were strong enough that he became a force to be reckoned with. The opposition hired a professional boxer to knock him out, but Pogy Bill knocked the pugilist out. This gave rise to the erroneous report that he was an Australian prizefighter.

It was 1910 when Pogy Bill signed on as a fisherman on Lake Okeechobee. This wild, rough calling—plus the frontier spirit and excel-lent pay—were natural attractions for this twenty-six-year-old man of the sea. It was not long before he owned his own fish camp and was rec-ognized as the undisputed top shark among the fishermen.

At that time, most fish camps had only tar-paper shanties with thatched roofs, but a rival camp owner invited Pogy Bill and his crew over to show off his new cypress wood camp. After the men consumed much of the victuals and drink provided for the occasion, they became cantankerous, and eventually a free-for-all fight broke out. Pogy Bill threw a rival right through one of the cypress walls. As others took up the fight, he threw them through a door, window, or wall, whichever was the handiest. When the last rival had been cleared from the room, a precariously hanging roof was all that remained of the cypress wood building.

No one was ever known to best Pogy Bill in a fair fistfight. Although he liked to drink, gamble, and fight—especially the latter— Pogy Bill had a code of fairness that Albert Berka, a Viennese immigrant, often attested to. Berka was the local baker, and more than once Pogy Bill came up with the restitution that kept him in business. Let me tell you about two of these incidents because they will give you a good picture of the type of justice meted out by Pogy Bill.

One day some soused fishermen robbed Berka's errand boy and ate or destroyed all the baked goods he was to deliver. Berka rushed to the scene, filled with indignation, but was completely ignored by the perpetrators of the crime. Then Pogy Bill appeared and demanded each of the fishermen pay Albert Berka $5 for the merchandise they had taken. With $25 in his pocket, Berka returned to his shop and replaced the orders.

Another time, in the wee hours of the night, Berka was awakened by some drunk, hungry fishermen pounding on his door. Against his better judgment, Berka agreed to get up and prepare something for them to eat but regretted his decision when the drunks decided to use his canned fruit for target practice. Streams of fruit juice were spewing in all directions when in walked Pogy Bill. "Now yuh gotta help Albert," Pogy Bill announced. "Will twenty-five dollars apiece pay for this mess?" he asked the baker. Before the destructive customers left the shop, Albert had $250 for his canned fruit.

Pogy Bill was usually in the forefront of the fishermen's fun and devilment. Once, when some of the lake men were arrested, their friends decided to have a little fun. When the prisoners were brought into court, which was being held in the back room of Dr. Darrow's drugstore, they disarmed the marshal and delayed Judge Hancock down the trail. Pogy Bill, barefoot as a yard dog, sat in the judge's chair, appointed Barefoot Jim as bailiff, and declared that court was now in session. As each accused man was brought before him, Pogy solemnly found him guilty, whether he was or not, and fined him one quart of liquor, to be produced at once. Then court was adjourned to Mr. Bryant's Roughhouse down at the creek.

Judge Hancock did not appreciate their humor and declared that the next time Pogy was brought before him, he would throw the book at him. Pogy sent word back to the judge that if he came before him, he would throw his honor into the lake. On Pogy Bill's next visit to town, he was waylaid on the Tantie Bridge by Judge Hancock and a couple of his deputies. As the creek was much handier than the lake, Pogy Bill threw all three of them into it.

Judge Hancock then deputized several of the most fearless cowhunters, traditional opponents of the fishermen. The next time Pogy Bill came into town, he was outmanned and locked up in the boxcar calaboose. Next morning, in a courtroom packed with belligerent fishermen, Pogy Bill was brought before Judge Hancock, who found him guilty of every kind of skulduggery in the statute book. As the judge pondered the heaviest sentence he could impose, he thumbed through a mail order catalog there on the druggist desk.

Expecting the worse, Pogy Bill exclaimed, "It's enough to be arrested for a little innocent fun, but I'll be dogged if I'm gonna be sentenced outten of a dadblamed Sears Roebuck catalog." And with that he overturned the table, spilling a pitcher of water into the judge's lap. This cost Pogy Bill $25 and ninety days in the Ft. Pierce jail.

Now, there are enough stories about Pogy Bill to keep telling them all night—many of them absolutely true, and some, no doubt, embellished. But I'm going to close now and invite you to join me when I tell you why Judge Hancock made a trip all the way to Ft. Pierce to see Pogy Bill. And why, many years later, a candidate for sheriff ran on the platform—"If I'm elected, I'll try to run this county the way Pogy Bill would want it to be run" —and won the election.

Telling time: 8–10 minutes
Audience: 4th grade–adult

Sheriff Pogy Bill

After I finished telling you my first episode about Pogy Bill, several of you asked me about his name.

"Anyone with the name William usually ends up being called Bill," you said. "But where and how did he get the nickname Pogy?"

That's a good question, and, as with the nickname Cracker, there are several answers. The explanation most often repeated is that Bill earned it when he tried to sell a boatload of pogies. Now, pogies are fish that are small and so full of bones that they are used only for bait or fertilizer. They are what is known in the trade as a trash fish, so it would be ludicrous to try to sell them to a fish dealer. I agree with several of his friends who insist that Pogy Bill was never that dumb. It seems to me that almost any man who had spent his life on the sea would have known better, and Pogy Bill was definitely a cut above the average. No, I believe that he came to be known as Pogy because someone likened him to those bony fish, which have a lot of strength and fight for their size. Pogy Bill was no big, lumbering catfish, nor was he a docile mullet. He was more like the feisty, bony pogies. At any rate, he got the name shortly after he became a fisherman and carried it to the pages of history. Even to this day he is known as Pogy Bill.

When we left off talking about Pogy Bill, he was in Ft. Pierce serving a ninety-day prison term, which Judge Hancock had sentenced him to. Being thrown in jail for ninety days might have come as a surprise to Pogy, but Judge Hancock was in for a surprise too. He was surprised to discover how many friends Pogy had, and all of them wanted him to commute Pogy's sentence. Members of the community, like Doc Anner (Dr. Anna Darrow) and her husband, exerted enough pressure that Judge Hancock agreed to go to Ft. Pierce and talk to the offender. Then the judge was in for an even bigger surprise. Pogy Bill agreed to give up his reckless fun and to help enforce the laws he had so often broken. The judge released him from jail, and Pogy Bill never broke his promise to Judge H. H. Hancock.

When Pogy Bill was released from prison and came back to Okeechobee City, it had been incorporated for nine months and had already lost two city marshals. There were no takers for third city marshal. Then Pogy Bill was offered and accepted the job. He was appointed city marshal on March 14, 1916, and held the job for the next two and a half years. Upon the death of Okeechobee County's first sheriff, Smith Drawdy, in 1918, Pogy Bill moved into the sheriff's office and remained there for the next fourteen years.

There has probably never been a sheriff who brought to the office a more comprehensive knowledge of the wily ways of lawbreakers than Pogy Bill. He knew all the nooks and crannies along the entire shoreline of Lake Okeechobee where the outlaws hid out. Only the foolish ever defied him. In the great 1928 hurricane, in which more than two thousand people perished, he was invaluable in identification since he knew everyone on the lake. When it was determined that he needed an assistant, he hired a rugged former Texas Ranger as his deputy. Deputy Charles Lee had fought with Teddy Roosevelt at the battle of San Juan Hill.

Pogy knew that any real improvements made in those around you had to start with you yourself. He gave up drinking and smoking and was soon married to a nice girl and settled into a new home. He collected a small library to begin a process of self-education, and once even took a fling at acting in a local amateur production of "Men's Flapper Chorus," staged as a benefit. Local ads urged readers to be sure to see "Pogy Bill's $1,000,000 legs."

Pogy not only cleaned up fighting, gambling, and other lawless activities, he saw the need for healthy outlets for energy and was soon organizing sports activities. He gently but firmly "coaxed" both natives and newcomers into joining and supporting the town's baseball team. Later he bought boxing gloves and taught boys how to box. When a Boy Scout troop was started in Okeechobee, it soon had Pogy Bill as an active troop leader. He also helped raise funds to keep the troop active.

Pogy's special concerns were children and the needy. It was said he never had a dime because he gave all his money away. Having no children of his own, he was the unofficial father of every orphan in the county. Every widow or family in distress was likely to find some groceries, clothes, or shoes on the doorstep, and everyone knew the anonymous party who had left them there.

In 1988, the late Wade Walker recalled with fondness the man he considered his friend. "I played on the ball team. . . . He thought the world of us boys. He took care of us just as though we were his own boys. He was a good man. He'd take us kids everywhere. . . . He had a big Lincoln. He'd load us up in his big car and take us with him and it never cost us a dime. If he knew of someone out there who didn't have anything to eat, he didn't ask them if they had anything. He'd just go into the store and buy a bunch of groceries and carry them out and set them on their steps. That's the kind of man he was."

In his *Cracker History of Okeechobee,* Lawrence Will quoted an old-timer: "Mister, I'm telling you what's so. For a heap of years, hit was Pogy Bill who kept Okeechobee County from going hongry."

In 1934, on the way to a fire, the fire truck overturned, pinning Pogy Bill beneath it. A few days later William E. Collins was dead. But Pogy Bill? Well, Lawrence Will continues his account:

"Not too long ago, whilst in a restaurant in Okeechobee, I heard a man a-telling how Pogy had influenced his early life, how he'd discouraged him from smoking cigarettes and drinking, how he'd found him jobs when he needed work, and how he'd get him to deliver packages to all them folks in need.

" 'I'm a-going to run for sheriff,' " this man declared. " 'There's things going on here that ain't just right. Now if you folks will elect me sheriff, I'll try to run this county the way that Pogy Bill would want it to be run!' "

He was elected!

Telling time: 8–10 minutes
Audience: 4th grade–adult

Fingy Conners

W ell, now, if you are a young sprout—that is, if you haven't celebrated at least sixty birthdays—chances are good you have never read the comic strip "Bringing Up Father." Between the 1920s and 1950s, George McManus created this comic strip, which appeared in more than 750 papers worldwide in 27 different languages. It spawned seven stage shows that toured the United States for eleven years, was dramatized on radio, and was made into a movie five times. There is no way of knowing how many tellers and writers were inspired by this popular real-life story.

It seems that when McManus was a young artist, he fell in love with the blond, beautiful daughter of the millionaire W. J. "Fingy" Conners. While Fingy had no objection to the proposed marriage, his society-minded spouse found that McManus was not on the social register and squelched the romance. But McManus got his revenge. In his comic strip, he gave Conners and his wife the names Jiggs and Maggie and was able to capture the essence of real people, which made the humor believable and endeared his comic characters to millions of readers. Okeechobee historians A. J. and Kathryn Hanna, after some research, concluded that the likeness between Fingy and Jiggs is startling. Fingy was a ringer for Jiggs, right down to his corned-beef-and-cabbage diet.

W. J. Conners started out life the hard way. At only thirteen, he was a cabin boy on a Great Lakes freighter. When he was big enough, he was a stevedore on the docks at Buffalo and got into a fistfight 'most every day. It was in one of these scuffles that he got the broken fingers that gave him the nickname Fingy. In time, by dint of honest toil and a little political finagling, Conners became boss of all the stevedores and soon made a fortune. It was then that "Maggie" dragged him to Florida to shine in the high society of Palm Beach.

In February 1917, Conners attended a swanky dinner celebrating the opening of the Palm Beach Canal and first heard about the Everglades. He couldn't stand still until he got a boat to take him to Lake Okeechobee. No sooner did he get there than he spent $40,000 for four thousand acres of sawgrass muck. And since Conners still had some money left, he bought the town site of Okeechobee and a few thousand acres of swamps and prairies thereabouts. Then, to round out his holdings, he bought all the lakeshore land still lying loose between Okeechobee and Canal Point. This twelve thousand acres cost him another $700,000.

Conners stood on the shore at Canal Point and exclaimed, "I own all the property from here slam to Okeechobee City, and yet I can't even get to the cussed land. Why, dagnabbit, I can't even set foot on the property to see what I've bought!" So he decided he'd build a road. He hightailed it up to Tallahassee, where the legislature was in session. It took the lawmakers two hours and twenty minutes to pass his highway bill. It authorized him to build a toll road from Twenty-Mile Bend on up to Okeechobee, nineteen miles of it along the Palm Beach Canal and thirty-three miles on soft muck that no such road had been built on before. Conners wanted the job finished yesterday, but he must have been pleased when such an undertaking was completed in eight month. On June 25, the road was opened and Conners began to collect tolls.

During construction, there had been much advertising and lots of ballyhoo. It paid off! The official opening of the highway was at Okeechobee on July 4, 1924. A motorcade of two thousand cars drove up from West Palm Beach, and every blessed one paid the $1.50 toll. Counting all the big shots and officials and all the cow hunters, cat fishers, and Seminoles, it was estimated that fifteen thousand people heard Governor Gary Hardee proclaim Fingy Conners to be a "great developer," comparable to Henry Flagler and Henry Plant. His highway was a "masterpiece of engineering," and Okeechobee, they all predicted, would now become the "Chicago of the South."

It was a grand celebration, but a torrential rain scattered the multitude, and Okeechobee lapsed into what it had been before, a cow town. When I checked last, it still had not become the "Chicago of the South." But, you know, it might have outshined Chicago if Fingy had lived to have gotten it done, but he died on October 5, 1929.

Telling time: 7–8 minutes
Audience: 4th grade–adult

Peggy O'Neale

M argaret O'Neale Eaton was the wife of Florida's territorial governor, John H. Eaton (1834–1836), a handsome man known for his integrity, ability, and congeniality. Gene Burnett, in the first volume of his *Florida's Past* series, gave an excellent thumbnail sketch of Margaret's most-eventful life: "As first lady, she reigned over Florida with the same sprightly zest and informality that had won her the admiration (and the unmerited censure) of the nation's capital city. . . . For Mrs. Eaton was none other than the attractive, witty, vivacious, former Peggy O'Neale, a vibrant figure in Washington circles before she was thirty; she had also been the object of gossip so scandalous that it caused a vice president to fall, a dark horse to succeed him, a national party to split, and an entire cabinet to resign. Disconcerting affairs, to say the least."

Margaret (Peggy) O'Neale was born December 3, 1799, in the first brick house built in Washington, D.C., which was much of a wilderness city at the time. Her mother, Rhoda, was a devout Methodist, and her father, William, a shrewd businessman whose Franklin House, offering rooms, food, and drink, became almost a second home for members of Congress and other dignitaries. At O'Neale's, they had the refuge of a cozy parlor, a genial host, a pretty, well-bred woman, and a charming child. That the family attracted many fastidious Congressmen was evident within a few seasons, when O'Neale had profited sufficiently to build an annex to his house.

Peggy was educated far beyond the station of an innkeeper's daughter. She went to the best school in the city, which the daughters of the most influential attended. The course of study embraced not only reading, writing, and arithmetic, but eleven other scholastic subjects as well as drawing, painting, and twenty-five different kinds of needlework. And to the young ladies who mastered these with dexterity, French, music, and dancing were taught.

Music and dancing were Peg's favorite studies. She so soon exhausted the dance teacher's repertoire that her father allowed her to have additional lessons with the expert dancing master, Mr. Generes. It was at the famous Union Tavern, the social center of the growing city, on March 16, 1812, that Mr. Generes gave his students' final ball for the season. Dolly Madison, the president's wife, accepted the invitation to judge the prestigious event and crown the Carnival Queen.

Peggy drove out with her parents and was in high feather. While others were nervously biting their nails, Peggy was eager to show her parents that they had not wasted money on her dance lessons. In her flounced white muslin dress, Miss Peggy O'Neale, with her clustering, rich brown curls, fair skin, and violet-blue eyes that fairly danced in time to her toes, was by far the prettiest girl present.

She seemed almost professional in the confidence of her movements; her dainty figure flew lightly through space; her pink-bowed satin slippers seemed barely to touch the floor. With each step, it was evident that she was leaving all her competitors far behind. With undisguised admiration, Mrs. Madison watched the precise patterns and the pleasing gestures of the child. As for pretty Peg—why, with Dad looking on, dance became all that was dear in life, and music the only language to hear. Unconsciously, she commanded attention; consciously, she held it. The judge saw her marshal an audience with a toss of her curls and dash like a dervish into a Highland Fling with a nicety that was a tribute to the trouble she took as well as to her talents. Unhesitatingly, Dolly Madison, the popular first lady, placed the Carnival Queen crown on Peggy's pretty head. Thus, at thirteen, Peggy O'Neal, by expended effort, natural ability, and inherent beauty, wrested from those who looked down on her as an innkeeper's daughter her first official social triumph.

Before she was fifteen, the trail of romances in her wake gave Peggy a certain distinction. On her account, the nephew of an acting secretary of the Navy had killed himself; two young army officers had passed a challenge to a duel; an elderly general was in a dither; and elopement with a major was prevented by her father, who then took Peggy to New York and enrolled her in a finishing school.

On her return to Franklin House, she could and would argue politics with the keenest wits, for she had developed a sharp, incisive mind. She knew by name every man of consequence in Washington and soon became a confidante of senators, congressmen, and Cabinet officers. Thus Peggy grew up in an atmosphere of political intrigue. She was beautiful, vivacious, and, against all the rules, intelligent. She was ultrafeminine yet preferred the company of men, which, along with her presence in a public house (even though it was her legitimate home), arched eyebrows and gave rise to every manner of bawdy speculation in a town where gossip and politics were almost synonymous.

At the age of sixteen, Peggy met John Timberlake, a handsome young purser in the U.S. Navy. Her parents approved of John, and after a whirlwind courtship, they were married. Maybe Timberlake, who was bothered with a pulmonary ailment, felt better when at sea. For whatever reason, he kept returning to sea, leaving Peggy and their children in Washington. Meanwhile, Andrew Jackson and John Henry Eaton, two O'Neale house visitors, became good friends of the family.

Eaton, Jackson's closest political confidante and friend, was one of the country's most distinguished senators. He was financially independent and an unfettered widower at twenty-eight. The youngest senator in the country had light auburn hair and large, expressive hazel eyes that were compassionate and steady. His figure was commanding, his countenance serene and dignified.

While Timberlake was at sea, Eaton escorted Margaret to official functions and took the entire family on carriage rides. Although the relationship was strictly proper, it fueled more town gossip. A year after Timberlake's death at sea, and just before Andrew Jackson took office as President, Margaret and John Eaton were married. That is when the rumor mill exploded. Gossip was spread by both men and women, from servants to the elite, bootblacks to clergymen, editors, and especially those holding political office. Her enemies wrote elaborate accounts of Peggy's transgressions and, in their attempts to damn her, often praised her. A lesser woman would have been unable to rise above such an all-out attack on her character. But Margaret Eaton kept a buoyant spirit and a good sense of humor.

Be it ever so hostile, there was no place like home for Peggy. She was a fighter, not a joiner, and Washington was her home. But she admitted that the Florida sunshine and flowers were a welcome reprieve from Washington's political thorns. Although Peggy was not pleased with the turn of events that sent her husband to Florida, she made the most of her reign as Florida's first lady. She cast aside social taboos and enjoyed lively political and social discussions with male guests. She spent much time and effort tutoring her two daughters. The climate was good for her health, and, breaking another taboo for the nineteenth-century woman, she often took her daughters swimming in the lake adjoining the governor's mansion. By accident, she discovered that a suntan enhanced her natural beauty and, thereafter, took daily sun baths at a time when no lady of quality went out without her parasol.

In 1836, President Jackson appointed Eaton ambassador to Spain. If Margaret Eaton was a fallen woman, she landed in a soft spot—as the beautiful wife of the much-admired ambassador to Spain. John Eaton's fine manners made an impression even on the Spanish Court, the most formal in Europe, and Peggy's radiant beauty captured the show wherever she went.

Margaret O. Eaton died on November 9, 1879, less than a month before her eightieth birthday. Among her last words were, "I am not afraid to die, but this is such a beautiful world to leave."

Telling time: 10–12 minutes
Audience: 4th grade–adult

Margaret Eaton's autobiography, which she dictated and proofread in 1873 with an understanding that it be published at a suitable time (Charles Scribner's Sons published it in 1932) closes with this statement: "I wish to leave this protest against the employment of slander for political purposes. I wish to beseech men and women, especially all who call and profess themselves to be Christians, to be careful how they repeat what they do not know to be true against men and especially against women. The men that started the slanders against me, which not yet have died out, have themselves died. They have gone to God. With God I leave them, quieting the bitterness of my heart with the remembrance of the solemn saying, 'Vengeance is mine. I will repay, sayeth the Lord.' It is hard to have suffered as I have, but if my blighted life can only warn men and women away from committing the crime of slander, if it can only lead men to cultivate that charity which I so sadly needed, then I shall not have lived in vain."

The three volumes of Gene Burnett's Florida's Past *(Pineapple Press) were used extensively in this story and are an excellent source of interesting tidbits to whet one's appetite for Florida's history.*

Smoking the Pipe of Peace

W hile John H. Eaton was Secretary of War (1829–1831), he was appointed, together with General Coffee, to a commission to make a treaty with the Indians. The Indians were so satisfied with the treaty and felt themselves so much indebted to Mr. Eaton, that they determined to make some exhibition of their gratitude. They offered him a tract of land in Florida, which it was said was worth $10,000. He steadfastly refused to accept it. But his grateful red brethren, determined not to let the business remain unfinished, arranged that they should call and pay their respects to Eaton and his wife, Margaret.

It was three o'clock one afternoon and Margaret was resting on the bed. Mr. Eaton entered and said, "Margaret, I want you to get up and send out and buy all the lemons there are in the District and make the largest quantity of lemonade that ever was made by hand."

Margaret looked at him and said, "Why, darling, are you beside yourself? What do you want all that for?"

Mr. Eaton said, "The Indians are coming to see us this evening, and I want you to entertain them."

Now, the Eatons' home was elegantly furnished, and Margaret took special pride in keeping it in perfect order. "I want no dirty, old, tobacco-smoking Indians in my parlors," she said.

"But, Margaret, this thing won't do you any harm. I have been making a treaty with them, and they are coming to our home, and we must treat our red brethren civilly."

"Oh, plague! Take your red brethren. Carry them off somewhere and take care of them yourself."

But Eaton coaxed his wife and pacified her so that she rose, sent out, and bought a quantity of lemons and two of the largest washtubs for sale in Washington. The washtubs were brought into the parlors and, when it was time for the red brethren to arrive, filled with enough lemonade to drown one or two of them.

Still Margaret was not happy about their visit. Just before they arrived, Eaton said, "Now, Margaret, you must be good and treat them nicely. And there is one thing more you will have to do—you will have to smoke the pipe of peace with them."

"What? No, never will I put one of their nasty pipes in my mouth!"

"Oh, you will have to do it. Because if you, the wife of the Secretary of War, refuse to smoke the pipe of peace, it will be construed as a declaration of hostilities, and we will have a terrible piece of work on hand."

Again, she vowed that not to save an all-out Indian war would she smoke their filthy pipes with them. But, as was his manner, her husband smoothed her feathers. At last, she said, "If I must, I'll carefully wipe the mouthpiece of the pipe with my handkerchief and take one whiff."

But Eaton solemnly assured her, "Unless you really want to bring on a bloody war, you must do no such indiscreet thing."

The Indians arrived. They were dressed in the most fantastic style of the forest and brought with them a little Indian boy. Margaret endured the salutations though she felt anything but cordial.

Colonel Reynolds, who was interpreter and in charge of the visit, stated that the Indians had brought the seven-year-old along as a gift. Margaret was quick to tell him that she certainly did not want an Indian child. She had children of her own. But Colonel Reynolds informed her that the Indians expected her to accept the boy, that he was a relative of John Ross, that the Eatons must provide for him. He concluded by saying, "He is a perfect Indian."

When it was made clear that they must accept the charge, Eaton graciously crossed his hands over the head of the boy and gave him the name John Henry Eaton Ross.

Margaret was really out of sorts now.

By and by, a servant came in with a great bundle in his arms wrapped in paper. It was received by Colonel Reynolds, who mounted a chair. The bundle was uncovered, and—lo and behold! —there was an elegant silver set, which in the name of the Indians Colonel Reynolds presented to Margaret, saying, "The chiefs have sought to make some expression of gratitude to Mr. Eaton for his kindness, and, as he will accept nothing at their hands, they have determined to bestow this upon his wife."

Eaton, who was standing by Margaret, whispered over her shoulder, "How about the red brethren now?"

To answer him, Margaret took two great silver pitchers from the hands of Colonel Reynolds, dipped them in the lemonade, and, lifting them as high as she could, saluted the red brethren and wished them all possible happiness. The gift pleased Margaret so much that she found the stomach not only to take one whiff of the pipe of peace but, in her enthusiasm, actually went around the circle and took the pipe out of each hand and gave it a whiff, as if she had been used to smoking all the days of her life.

The little fellow took to his new parents with all his affection, and, in spite of the fact that he often betrayed traces of his early forest training, Mr. Eaton, Margaret, and her daughters became very fond of John Henry. He stayed with his adoptive parents three years. During a family trip to Nashville, as they were crossing a river, John jumped into the river with a splash and struck out for shore. It was a simple feat for him because he had been accustomed to swimming across the Potomac River.

When Mr. Eaton saw the boy swimming away from them, he refused to recover him. Whether from an Indian or a white man, ingratitude was not acceptable to him, and he said, "Let him go. Let him go!"

Mr. Eaton contacted nearby residents and asked them to take care of the boy's needs, but John found his people and made good his escape. He was a handsome boy and, as Colonel Reynolds had said, a perfect Indian.

Telling time: 5–6 minutes
Audience: 4th grade–adult

Introduction

Tall Tales and Nonsense Stories

T he primary purpose for telling a story should always be to entertain. The art of storytelling is first, last, and always an art of entertainment. If there is anything this world needs, it is more laughter. And the stories here are guaranteed to produce a belly laugh. These are the stories that are the most entertaining when they're told rather than read.

And, remember, the successful teller of tall tales and nonsense stories not only needs to learn the story line but also to control his own laughter. The teller who tells a riotous story with a poker face makes his tale all the more hilarious!

Do Tell!

Book-Learnt

I f terrorists had not bombed the imperial dining room of the winter palace in St. Petersburg, Russia, the city of St. Petersburg, Florida, might never have been born. For it was this act of violence in 1880 that caused Peter W. Demens, a prince from an old aristocratic Russian family, to leave his homeland and bring his family to settle in Longwood, Florida. Evidently, Peter bought acreage there, for about a year later, in lieu of payment for $9,400 worth of cross-ties, Demens was given the financially defunct Orange Belt Railroad, which ran from Sanford to Apopka. With a railroad and no money, Demens used the railroad as collateral and formed the Orange Belt Investment Company with the express purpose of building a railroad from the St. Johns River near Sanford to Pinellas Point on the Gulf. Here, Peter Demens named the terminal St. Petersburg, after his hometown in Russia. By November 1886, the Orange Belt Investment Company had its first train rolling into the town of Oakland, west of Orlando.

Speaking of Oakland, let me tell you about Henry and MaryBeth Perkins, who lived out that way. They had one boy, Henry Jr. —everyone called him Hank. Before he was dry behind the ears, Henry and MaryBeth started selling off their virgin timber so they could send him all the way to Virginia to school. After seven years, he schooled out and came home. Now Henry and MaryBeth were powerful proud of him, they wus, and they had every right to be. After all, they had the only boy 'round that was book-learnt, and furthermore he had outdone all his classmates in somethin' called al-*gee*-bra, whatever that be. They stayed up till nearly nine o'clock the night that Hank got home, listening to him tell the amazing stories of college life, and they invited all their kith and kin, friends and neighbors from near and far, for dinner on Sunday to show off Hank and to share all this wonderment with them.

Saturday morning, Henry and MaryBeth were up early—cookin',

feedin' up, and milkin'. They had a young cow that had never been to the pail before, and, when MaryBeth tried to milk her, she started kicking.

MaryBeth called, "Henry, come here quick, and help me with this here crazy cow. I need the milk fer the cookin' today."

Henry came to the cow lot and tried to hold the cow, but she kept on rearin' and a-pitchin' and kickin' over the milk pail. Henry said to MaryBeth, "We don't need to strain and struggle with this here cow. We got a son inside that's been off to school fer seven years and done learnt everything. He'll know just what to do with a kickin' cow. Ah'll go call him." He called Hank and told him their problem.

The boy came out to the cow lot and looked everything over good. Then he said, "Mama, cow kickin' is all a matter of scientific principle. You see, before a cow can kick she has to hump herself up in the back. So all we need to do is to take the hump out of the cow's back."

"But, son, ah don't see how you're goin' ter do that. But 'course you been off to college, and you know a heap more than me and yore pa will ever know. We'll be mighty 'bliged to ye if you can take the hump out of the heifer."

Hank put on his gold-rimmed eyeglasses and studied the cow from head to foot. Then he said, "All we need to keep this animal from humping is a weight on her back."

"What kinda weight, son?" Henry asked

"Oh, any kind of weight, just so it's heavy enough, Papa," said Hank. "It's just plain mathematics."

"Where we goin' ter git any mathematic weight like that, son?"

"Why don't you get up there, Papa? You're just about the weight we need."

"Son, you've been off to school a long time, and maybe you done forgot how hard it is for a body—anybody—to sit on a cow! And ah'm gittin' old, you know."

"But, Papa, I can fix that too. I'll tie your feet together under her belly so she can't throw you. You just get on up there."

"All right, son, if you say so, ah'll get straddle of this here cow. You know more'n ah do, ah reckon."

So they tied the cow up short to a tree, and, after an agonizing struggle, Henry managed to get on. Hank passed the rope under the cow's belly and tied his papa's feet together. Again, MaryBeth tried to milk the cow, but that cow had other notions. She kept buckin' and rearin' so till Henry felt he couldn't stand it no more.

He hollered to Hank, "Cut the rope, son, cut the rope! Ah wants to git down."

Hank started trying to cut the rope, but the cow was acting up so that instead of cutting the rope that tied his papa's feet, he cut the rope that tied the cow-brute to the tree, and she lit out across the weeds with Henry on her back with his feet tied under her belly.

The cow and Henry went bustin' on down the back road till they met a neighbor. She was surprised to see Henry ridin' a cow.

She called out, "My Lawd, Brother Henry, where are you goin'?"

"Sister Bidell, not even mah book-learnt son knows the answer to that question. For only God and this crazy cow knows where ah'm a-goin'."

At last the cow was hemmed up and Hank managed to cut the rope and get his papa on his feet. Although Henry was pretty shook up, he moved around as naturally as possible with no complaints. He didn't want to remind anyone of this happening. The incident tended to tarnish his pride.

On Sunday, tables were set up under the Chinaberry trees and loaded with mouthwatering victuals. Folk buzzed around like flies around a molasses barrel. When the parson put an "Amen" on the food blessin', everyone started feedin' his face, and there was a lull in conversation.

Henry said, "Son, why don't you say somethin' in al-*gee*-bra for us?"

"Papa, let's just enjoy all this good-tastin' food?"

"We can enjoy the food while you say somethin' in al-*gee*-bra."

"I'm sure, Papa, that these folks would rather hear one of your stories than my algebra."

"Son, ah'm not one bit slow to admit that ah'm mighty proud of what you've done—showin' them college professors that yore head ain't jest a knot to keep yore spinal cord from unravelin'—so go ahead and say somethin' in al-*gee*-bra for all of us."

Hank didn't want to disappoint or embarrass his papa. He racked his brain as to what to say. At last he was inspired and said, "Pi r square, pi r square, pi r square." Pleased with how he had risen to the occasion, he looked at his papa for his approval, but Henry had a long face and downcast eyes.

"No, son, you've been off to school so long and worried yore head over that al-*gee*-bra so much that you've done plum forgot—pie are round, cornbread are square!"

Telling time: 9–10 minutes
Audience: 4th grade–adult

Historical notes for this story were taken from Volume 1 of Gene Burnett's Florida's Past *(Pineapple Press, 1996).*

Dogbone

You know, my Uncle Orson is usually as warm and friendly as a little hound puppy and as invitin' as a cup of coffee when it's been saucered and blowed, but I was by his place a few days ago and found him as standoffish as a sore-tail cat at a rockin' chair convention. But Uncle Orson is always up front and lets you know what's ailin' him.

He spoke right up. "Sanky, Tildie tells me that you're jest a runnin' all over the place tellin' stories these days."

"Actually, Uncle Orson, I didn't seek any gigs for this spring so I have less storytelling to do than usual."

"I understood Tildie to say that you were telling at the Ocala Storytelling Festival and Gamble Rogers Folk Festival and you always go up to White Springs to tell for the State Folk Festival. Sounds to me like you are crackin' pretty good."

"I always look forward to each one of the festivals."

Unc's gray eyes turned steel blue and his long beard started bobbin' up and down like it does when he gets upset about something. "Tildie says you're not sayin' a word about Dogbone."

"No! Uncle Orson, you've convinced me not to say anything about Dogbone."

"I don't want you gettin' a bunch of drifters or developers in here, but when you get a nice audience, you could tell 'em a little bit about Dogbone."

Since you are such a nice audience and I need to keep peace in the family, let me tell you a little bit about Dogbone. I can't tell you much for there jest ain't much to tell, 'cause Dogbone is jest a wide spot on Sandspur Road in what used to be Mosquito County. Uncle Orson says that changing that county's name to Orange was the biggest whitewash job the Florida politicians ever pulled off. They do have mosquitoes there. Uncle Orson says that they can sing louder and harmonize better than the Mormon Tabernacle Choir. Aunt Matilda says that Orson makes too much of a to-do about the mosquitoes for she hasn't had a single mosquito at her place in months. When Uncle Orson heard her say that he said that he hadn't had a single one at his place either—every one of them is married and has dozens of kids! Of course, Aunt Matilda declares that even the mosquitoes in Dogbone are religious, and Uncle Orson agrees with her. He says, "They're religious, all right. They sing over you and prey on you!"

I mustn't get started telling you Uncle Orson's mosquito stories because I must tell you about Dogbone. It has a few houses in it, a bar-B-Q stand with a gas pump out front, a beer joint, and a Methodist Church. My Aunt Matilda lives right there in Dogbone, and after you pass her house the road starts up a hill—a rather steep one for Florida. The first house on your right belongs to Ed Grady, the town drunk. At least, he was until about a month ago, when he was converted. Uncle Orson says that now they don't have a town drunk—everyone just has to take his turn. As you go on up the road, on your left is the Williams place. They have an old rusted-out pickup truck on cement blocks out in their front yard and a parcel of dogs that like to chase cars. Right at the top of the hill is Uncle Orson's mailbox. Actually he lives about two miles off the road on a nice little muck farm. It's a small farm but it is all paid for, and, gals, Uncle Orson is not married. I'm not sure just how old he is—he won't say—but he declares he's going to live another hundred years. And, you know, he might do it, because he eats the right food, gets plenty of exercise and sleep, and recently he stumbled on a guard against the mosquitoes. It was right after Halloween when Uncle Orson stopped in at the Cheapo Depot. Among their many big sale items was fluorescent body lotion. Because of his curiosity and weakness for bargain, Uncle Orson bought a couple of bottles. That night he rubbed some of the lotion on his arms and hands before going out to sit in his porch swing and discovered that, although it only glowed a little in the dark, it kept the mosquitoes at bay. He went back the next day and bought the six cases that the Cheapo Depot had. Uncle Orson prefers to sleep in the nude, and this lotion gave him the chance to not be bothered with cumbersome nightclothes and still not be bitten by mosquitoes.

Well, that's about all there is to tell you about Dogbone, except it wouldn't be right to mention Ed Grady's conversion and not tell you how it happened. There are several versions floating around Dogbone and I've listened to them all. My version is based both on facts and hearsay, but to the best of my knowledge and belief this is what actually happened on Friday the thirteenth.

Uncle Orson had already applied the fluorescent skin lotion to his entire body and was about to retire for the night when he remembered that he had failed to pick up his mail that day. He thought about just leaving it until the next day, but he knew that with something like that on his mind he wouldn't sleep a wink, so he decided to go on and get it. It was a warm night and he figured he wouldn't see anyone and, more importantly, no one would see him, so he'd go on just as he was. He stepped into a pair of shoes and started out. The moon hadn't come up yet and it was a dark night, so Uncle Orson went back into the house for a light. He doesn't own a regular flashlight, but he does have a froggin' light that works off of a battery. A froggin' light is much like a miner's light except it is held on your forehead with one strap over your head and one around your head.

He got into his pickup, drove up to Sandspur Road, headed the truck toward Dogbone, pulled up his parking brake, left the motor running, and got out. He adjusted the light on his forehead and turned it on only to find that the battery was about dead and instead of the light shining it just glowed. But with the help of the truck lights, he found his mailbox, and, just as he got his hands full of all those sales papers and seed catalogs, he thought that his truck was moving. He turned around and found that he was right. He had meant to get that parking brake fixed but he hadn't got around to it. Now all he could do was try to overtake his truck.

He started running down the hill after it. The Williams's dogs were surprised to see Uncle Orson out chasing cars, but they were glad enough to join him in the chase. The truck gained speed as it went down the hill, but so did Uncle Orson. In fact, he almost caught it but just then he stumbled over one of the dogs.

Now, staggering up from the beer joint was Ed Grady—drunk again! He saw the light of the truck coming toward him and stumbled off the road to let it pass. When it went by, he wasn't sure but he thought the cab was empty. He staggered back onto the road, trying to figure that out, when he heard the dogs barking. He turned around and saw coming toward him a tall glowing figure with a white beard bobbing in the breeze and only one eye—right in the middle of his forehead. Just that afternoon, his wife had told Ed if he didn't mend his ways the devil was coming for him. At the time he had laughed it off, but now he reconsidered her warning, turned around and started running. The dogs were excited about someone else joining the chase and started barking louder. Ed Grady was sure they were hell hounds and figured that the only way he would ever again see the light of day was to outrun them. He increased his speed. He caught up with the truck. When he did, Orson bellowed out, "Get in the truck!" Ed Grady took one look and saw that the truck was indeed empty, and again he picked up his speed. He led the procession into Dogbone. He made a long sliding dive up under the first building that he came to, and up under that building he stayed.

The truck slowed down when it got on level ground and came to a stop in Aunt Matilda's compost pile. Uncle Orson was in it in a minute and drove off with the dogs following, still barking. After everything got quiet, Ed Grady cautiously crawled out and looked around. He found that he had been under the Methodist Church. Well, he took this as a sign, and the very next Sunday he joined the church and has been a faithful member ever since.

If any of you are ever over in that neck of the woods, stop by and hear Aunt Matilda's, Ed's, or Uncle Orson's version, but be sure you tell Uncle Orson that I told you a little bit about Dogbone.

Telling time: 8–10 minutes
Audience: adults

BeeBeeBumpkin

It was late summer of 1838 when his pappy passed on, leaving BeeBeeBumpkin and his coonhound, Chipper, as the lone caretakers of the homestead located near the headwaters of the Chipola River. As BeeBeeBumpkin painstakingly gathered the last scraps of cotton from the now-brown cotton bowls, he made up his mind that he was going to do a little traveling. Never in his sixteen years had he been beyond the forks in the river, and every week the copy of the *St. Joseph Times* arrived with its colorful descriptions of this fabulous city. According to the paper, the population of St. Joseph now numbered six thousand, making it the largest city in Florida. BeeBeeBumpkin had read every word of the *St. Joseph Times* to his pappy, after his eyes failed him and before he died. They enjoyed hearing how Apalachicola would not give up the county seat, so those folks in St. Joseph formed Calhoun County and made St. Joseph its county seat. But Pappy warned that the folks in Apalachicola might have some ammunition in their accusations that St. Joseph was "the wickedest city in America."

But the more stories BeeBeeBumpkin heard about the horse track, casino gambling in every hotel, plain and fancy houses of ill-repute, saloons, floating con games, and prizefights, the more he wanted to see it for himself. And when he read the latest copy of the *St. Joseph Times,* which told about St. Joseph being chosen to host the territory's first constitutional convention and about a gala celebration that would welcome Florida's most prominent leaders on December 3, 1838, he lost no time in getting ready to leave. He hid the ax and large skillet. He put the small skillet, some fat, sweet potatoes, meal, and salt in a croaker sack, got his fishing line, put out the fire, hung a flask of shot and his powder horn around his neck, took down Ole Sure-fire, called up Chipper, and was on his way.

He walked over the hill and a good piece further until he came to the crossroads. He took the sack from his shoulder, got out a sweet "tater," broke it open, put some of the hog fat in it, and gave it to Chipper, who gulped it down and begged for another one.

"Chip, that's 'nough for you right now. I want you to listen to me, boy. It's not that I don't enjoy yore company, for I do, but I think for yore sake you'd better stay with Cozen Chicane while I'm gone. I'll stop for you on my way back home." He and Chipper went on to Cozen Chicane's house. He knocked on the door. Cozen Chicane came to the door and stuck his nose out the crack.

"Who's there?" he asked, not daring to come out for fear it was somebody he'd beat in some sorta deal.

"It's me, BeeBeeBumpkin. Just me and my hound dog, Chipper."

Cozen Chicane opened the door then and gave BeeBeeBumpkin a sly look. "Come in and rest a bit and eat a bite," he said, although he was hoping that BeeBeeBumpkin wouldn't. He was a fat man who was always grinning like a mule eating briars and always easy talking, like butter wouldn't melt in his mouth. But he was just about the slickest, double-dealingest old cooter in the country or anywhere else, for that matter. Nobody could beat him in a deal—least-wise, they never had. And when it came to lawin', Cozen Chicane was always suing somebody.

"Why don't you come in, BeeBeeBumpkin?" he said.

"Because I'm on my way, Cozen Chicane. I'm a-going to town for sure. It's forty miles and across two counties, but I aim ter see that town. That's why I come to see you."

Cozen Chicane started shutting the door. "Now, now, BeeBeeBumpkin," he said. "I'm hard up for money right now. I couldn't loan my sweet mother—may God rest her soul—so much as a penny."

"I don't want no money," said BeeBeeBumpkin. "I ain't the borrowing kind."

So Cozen Chicane poked his head out again. "What can I do for you then?"

"Well, it's like this. The way Ma figured it, you're my thirty-second cousin twice removed, my only kin in this world. I got a favor for you to do for me."

Cozen Chicane started pushing that door shut. "No, no favors. I make it a rule to do no favors and don't expect none from nobody."

"It's a favor I'm aiming to pay for," said BeeBeeBumpkin.

"Oh," said Cozen Chicane, opening the door once more, "that's different now. Come right in, BeeBeeBumpkin."

"No, sir, no need to come in, for I'd just get in my way coming out. What I want you to do is keep my coonhound, Chipper, while I'm off on my travels. I'll pay what's right when I come back to get him."

Cozen Chicane grinned all over, more than anywhere else, as he thought he saw a way to make something extra or get himself a coonhound. Everybody knew BeeBeeBumpkin was simple-minded—honest as the day's long but simple-minded.

"Why, yes," said Cozen Chicane, "I'll keep Chipper for you, BeeBeeBumpkin, and glad to."

So BeeBeeBumpkin gave his hound dog over and bid Cozen Chicane farewell. "I'll be back next week or month or sometime. I don't know how long it'll be, for it's forty miles and across two counties to town."

Well, one day, week, or month after that, BeeBeeBumpkin reached the city of St. Joseph. It was a sight for him to see, and he looked and looked until he was plum tired of lookin'. He decided there weren't one thing there that he couldn't go home without. The next day, he took the same road that got him there and started back home. Sometime after that, here came BeeBeeBumpkin down the pike-road to the crossroads, limping and dusty. He went straight to Cozen Chicane's house and knocked on the door.

Cozen Chicane stuck his nose out the crack and said, "Who's there?"

"It's me, BeeBeeBumpkin."

"How are you, BeeBeeBumpkin?"

"Fair to middling. I walked to town and saw it all and then walked back here again. Forty miles and across two counties, both ways. Don't never want to roam no more. I'm satisfied now."

Cozen Chicane started shutting the door. "Glad to hear it, BeeBeeBumpkin. Next time you come down to the crossroads, drop in and say hello. Any time, just any time, BeeBeeBumpkin."

"Hold it right there! Wait a cotton-pickin' minute!" said BeeBeeBumpkin, putting his foot in the door.

"I'm busy," said the old man.

But BeeBeeBumpkin kept his foot in the door. "How about Chipper, Cozen Chicane? How about him?"

Cozen Chicane kept trying to shut the door and BeeBeeBumpkin kept shoving his foot in to prevent him from doing it. "See here!" said BeeBeeBumpkin, "I'm here to get my coonhound."

"Oh, him? Why, I declare to my soul, I'd almost forgot about that hound dog, BeeBeeBumpkin, I sure almost had."

"Where's he at?" asked BeeBeeBumpkin, still keeping the old man from closing the door.

"I'll tell you," said Cozen Chicane, still trying to shut the door, "I feel mighty bad about it, BeeBeeBumpkin, but your Chipper is no more."

"What do you mean he is no more? How come?"

"Jest that he's perished and gone, BeeBeeBumpkin. The first night after you left I sort of locked him up in that little busted-down house over in the Old Ground. Just to keep him safe, you know? Well, sir, BeeBeeBumpkin, those last renters of mine that lived there was powerful dirty folks. They left the place just lousy with chinch bugs. Them bugs was mortal hungry by this time. So they just et that dog of yours alive. Et all but the poor thing's bones by morning—and even the bones was purty well gnawed.

"It was my fault in one way. I ought to known better than to put your dog in there, BeeBeeBumpkin. But I done it, believin' it wus the right thing ter do. But I'm not goin' to charge you a penny for his keep the night I had him. I aim to do the fair thing."

Well, Cozen Chicane stuck his sly eye to the crack of the door to see how BeeBeeBumpkin was taking it. He knew the boy was simple-minded. He figured he had him. Cozen Chicane had Chipper hid out, and he aimed to swap him to a man he knew in the next county.

BeeBeeBumpkin had learned to accept death when he had done all he could to keep it from happening, but now he blamed himself for leaving Chipper. He stood there, his heart wrenched. Tears came in his eyes and he sleeved his nose. "That dog was folks to me," he said. "Them chinch bugs don't know what they done to me." He pulled his foot out of the door and backed down the steps and started towards home. Cozen Chicane eased out onto the porch to watch him go.

About this time, BeeBeeBumpkin turned around. "Cozen Chicane," he said, with tears still in his voice, "my place is over the hill and a good piece further on. I'm plum tired out and beat. Wonder if you'd loan me your mule to ride on. I'll bring it back tomorrow."

The old man was tickled with how he'd got him a good hound to swap without it costing him anything, and he knew BeeBeeBumpkin was honest as the livelong day, so he just called across the way to the crossroads store and got a witness to the loan and let BeeBeeBumpkin take the mule.

Next morning, BeeBeeBumpkin never showed up and Cozen

Chicane got worried. He got worrieder still in the middle of the day when no sign of BeeBeeBumpkin did he see. But along about afternoon he saw BeeBeeBumpkin come walking over the hill and down towards the crossroads. Cozen Chicane ran out onto his porch and yelled, "Hey, BeeBeeBumpkin, where's my mule?"

BeeBeeBumpkin just shook his head and kept walkin'. "I feel mighty bad about that mule, Cozen Chicane," he called. "I sure do."

"Hey! Wait there!"

But BeeBeeBumpkin went on, heading for the store at the crossroads.

Cozen Chicane was so mad he didn't wait to put on his shoes. He just jumped off the porch and ran to that good old man's house up the road a-ways.

"Squire," he said, "I want you to handle BeeBeeBumpkin. He stole my mule."

The Squire waked up his deputy and the deputy went down and brought in BeeBeeBumpkin. Everybody at the crossroads come tagging along behind.

Squire said, "Son, they tell me you stole a mule."

"No, sir, Squire, I never done it," said BeeBeeBumpkin.

Cozen Chicane stomped his bare feet, shook his fists, and yelled, "He's a bald-faced liar!"

"Calm down, Cozen Chicane," said the Squire, "and let the boy tell his side. Go ahead, BeeBeeBumpkin."

So BeeBeeBumpkin told how he borrowed the mule and started for home. "Well," he said, "you know I live over the hill and a good piece further. I rode that mule to the top of the hill. I was minding my own business and not giving nobody any trouble. Then, all of a sudden, I see a turkey buzzard dropping down outen the sky. Here it come, dropping fast and crowing like a game rooster.

"First thing I knew that old buzzard just grabbed Cozen Chicane's mule by the tail and gave it a hard yank and that mule's hind legs lifted off the ground, and I went flying over his head and hit a rock head-on. I failed in my senses for a minute. When I could see straight, I saw that buzzard sailing away with the mule, 'most a mile high and getting littler all the time. And that's how it happened. I sure am sorry, but there ain't much you can do with a thing like that, Squire."

"Hold on there!" said Squire Jowers, that good old man. "I've seen many a turkey buzzard in my time, BeeBeeBumpkin, but never have I seen one that could crow."

"Well," said BeeBeeBumpkin, "it surprised me some too. But in a county where chinch bugs can eat up a full-grown hound dog in one night, why, I just reckon a turkey buzzard has a right to crow and fly off with a mule if he wants to."

So it all come out and Squire Jowers, that good old man, made Cozen Chicane fork up Chipper and then BeeBeeBumpkin gave back the mule. Cozen Chicane was mocked and branded. He was so ashamed that he grieved and pined away, and it weren't no more than fifteen or twenty years before he was taken sick and died.

Telling time: 18–20 Minutes
Audience: 4th grade–adult

I hope this story will whet the appetite of every reader to learn more about Florida's mystery city. As Gene Burnett recalls in Volume 2 of Florida's Past, *"St. Joseph mushroomed overnight—booming, flamboyant, and wicked—and for several years it remained the metropolis queen of Florida. But almost as suddenly, the thriving seaport town of St. Joseph disappeared from the face of the earth, obliterated by yellow fever, fire, and a hurricane."*

The long, descriptive names and repetition in this story give it a certain rhythm and down-home charm, which will be lost if you shorten or replace the names with pronouns.

Introduction

Stories for Special Days

S tories are such an integral part of a celebration that even though there is a large supply of holiday stories, there is an even larger demand for them. A story that a Cracker can relate to, enjoy, and share for the celebration of each of three major holidays—Christmas, Thanksgiving and Halloween—is included as well as one for the lesser-observed April Fool's Day. Stories nurture appreciation and understanding so enjoy and share these and other stories. Celebrate special days with thankful hearts and appreciative spirits.

Do Tell!

First, Consider the Cost

S ome sage from age: Jokes are best talked about but never carried
out.

Recently, on the evening news, I heard that a man lost his job because
he played a practical joke on his supervisor. I was filled with empathy for
the culprit. As one of seven children who created most of their own entertainment, I was often either the perpetrator or the butt of a practical joke.
I learned early to give and take, but it wasn't until I was a sophomore in
high school that a practical joke backfired and I learned that not all givers
are takers and that a practical joke can have costly repercussions.

It was Sunday afternoon, the last day of March, when my sister
made some caramel-coconut kisses and brought them out to the porch
to treat the family. As we savored the candy, Daddy asked, "Did you
know that if you add sugar to Octagon laundry soap, it will take away
the odor?"

I've often wondered where my father got that bit of information.
My dad enjoyed a good joke as much as anyone I've ever known, and I
am sure he was aware that the next day was April Fool's Day, but I am
doubly sure that he had no intention of getting me in trouble. What he
had said was news to me, and it didn't take me long to figure out a way
to make use of this new bit of knowledge.

With my last coconut–caramel kiss wrapped in wax paper, I went
looking for laundry soap. Out in the laundry shed I found some soap
scraps that I knew would not be missed. I noticed that there was no
noticeable difference between the color of the soap and that of the
caramel candy. I made quick work of scraping the soap into a small dish
and adding a bit of sugar. I was delighted to find that the sugar not only
removed the soap's odor but also gave it the right consistency to pass for
candy. A sprinkling of coconut made it a bit dry so I added a drop of

vanilla, then shaped three candy kisses on wax paper. I was all set for April Fool's Day on Monday.

I thought the deception was perfect and went back to the porch swing to ponder who was worthy to be the butt of such a great practical joke. It didn't take me long to come up with the perfect candidate, my homeroom teacher. He was popular with the student body and a close friend of my basketball coach. He helped drive the team to all out-of-town games, so I often rode in his car. He teased me relentlessly, which I accepted good-naturedly because I thought he liked me (I never teased anyone I didn't like).

On Monday as I walked to school, I was hailed by a classmate, "Hey, wait up." As he walked up, I nibbled on my caramel candy and offered him some of the soap candy. He took one piece, bit into it, and was immediately wise to the deception. I said, "April Fool!" We both laughed and carefully arranged the soap candy back on the wax paper for our teacher.

When we reached school, he stopped in the hall to let some of his friends in on the joke. Our teacher had already seen us walking together and started making some remarks about how spring produced strange love affairs. I interrupted his bantering to ask if he wanted a piece of candy.

"Sure," he said and carefully scraped the wax paper clean, threw back his head, and dropped the three soap kisses into his mouth, then proceeded to lick his fingers. I could no longer keep a straight face so I turned and walked to my desk. After what seemed a very long time, I decided that he was actually going to eat the sweetened soap and the joke would be on me.

Just as I turned to see what was going on, he realized that he was the victim of a joke and rushed to the window to spit the soap out. Then he ran to the water fountain. The soap formed so many suds that he kept foaming at the mouth and the suds kept covering his face. This kept the other students in stitches until the assembly bell rang. In assembly, he started reading the morning devotions but had to stop three times to remove bits of soap from his mouth. Each time he did this, it provoked another outburst of laughter from the student body.

After the third time, he looked at me and said, "Young lady, I'm going to get even with you, and when I do even your mama won't know you!"

Everyone, at times, wishes for hindsight wisdom. Many were the times I bemoaned the fact that I didn't have an inkling of what shallow water I was diving into, playing a practical joke on someone who had the upper hand. For the rest of that semester and the next two, he ignored rules of ethics to make good his threat. I had to fight tooth and nail to get the grades I earned in both of his classes. But, even more devastating, I had lost a friend. For many years, I regretted that my April Fool joke had proved so costly. But in light of the evening news and the fact that years later my teacher regretted his poor sportsmanship and we became friends again, maybe it was a good long-term investment. It taught me the truth in the admonition to first consider the cost.

Telling time: 8–10 minutes
Audience: 4th grade–adult

I have found that audiences enjoy the humor of this personal, true story and the chance to use the story as a window into Florida culture more than six decades ago. If you are a young teller or a newcomer to Florida and you want to tell it in the first person, preface the story by saying, "I have a friend who has lived in Florida for a long, long time, and she shared this story with me. She gave me permission to share it with you. . . ."

Forever Thankful

"Today, tradition dictates that I tell the first story. If you will indulge me, I would like to preface my story with a few observations and remarks. First, I'd like to quote my PaPa and endorse his words when he said: "All of y'all are as welcomed as fresh biled coffee after it's been saucered and blowed." With these words my grandfather opened the storytelling session that followed our Thanksgiving dinner.

"As long as my grandparents lived here on the west bank of the Kissimmee River," he continued, "each member of their extended family was devoted to being here every Thanksgiving at high noon. It was then that the dinner bell was rung twelve gongs, one for each month of the year, and PaPa, with his powerful voice, said, 'Let's again give thanks.'

"If there are any of you who have never been a participant in an old-time Southern family gathering, it is hard for you to imagine the camaraderie engendered, the number of people, or the amount and variety of food involved. From the time I was old enough to gather buttonwood and cut and weave moonvine, I've felt like an integral part of these annual celebrations, and the fondest memories of my life are centered around them.

"The old home-place burned, and for three years now we have failed to observe this family's old tradition. I don't know about you, but for three years I have felt that a light in my life has been snuffed out. But as each of you arrived at our new home this year, you helped rekindle that light. It is now burning brightly, and I thank you for that.

"But you've asked me to tell you about my most memorable Thanksgiving celebration. I had no trouble deciding which one that was. It had to be the one we observed the year that I was sixteen. That was the year I met the love of my life and also learned that I should not only be thankful for the fortunate things that come my way but be truly grateful for being spared the destructive ones, which, but for the grace of God, might have been my lot in life.

"I am sure that some of you are giving thought to some of PaPa's stories, trying to recall one that would have taught a lovesick teenager such a spiritual truth. Like most of you, I learned many lessons from PaPa's stories, but this lesson I learned from Uncle Si.

"For the benefit of the youngsters in our midst and any of you who never knew him, let me introduce you to Uncle Si. I think his name was Silas, but I never heard him called anything but Uncle Si. As far as I know, he was not a bona fide member of our family, but PaPa was known for his hospitality to family, friends, and strangers, so, for as many years as I can remember, as long as he lived, Uncle Si, with his fiddle, was a regular participant at our family celebrations.

"It seems that before Uncle Si had sprouted his pin feathers, his father was killed during a fracas while he was fiddling in the DoseDo Sisters' newly constructed dance hall. It was the consensus that it was an accident—just a stray bullet—but he was just as dead as if someone had been gunning for him.

"His grieving mother did not want Si to play the fiddle so she sold the instrument to the DoseDo Sisters. They paid her top dollar, although neither of them could play a lick. This transaction helped convince folks of the truth in the scuttlebutt—that they often sampled their supply of medicinal moonshine.

"When the flu took Si's mother, the sisters took Si. I don't think they even considered adopting him, but they gave him a foster home and let him practice on the fiddle. It was not long before he was known as the best fiddler in that neck of the woods. Of course, I don't know that he had much competition. But if you ever heard Uncle Si play, you knew that fiddle was in the hands of its master.

"But times got hard. Folks still said, 'The fiddler must be paid,' but the pine-needle basket no longer harvested a handful of dimes and a quarter or two. Si's evening of playing would yield only a nickel or maybe two and a few pennies.

"When Si was twelve years old, he was tall for his age, and, although he didn't have enough fat on his bones to grease a one-egg skillet, he was strong and willing to work. He got a job with one of the many seining crews fishing Lake Okeechobee. He didn't mind the work, and he was one more happy kid when he got his first pay. The first thing he did was to buy back his father's fiddle. Once the fiddle was his, the two seemed to meld and his playing was better than ever. His music reflected his joy for he was happier than he could remember ever being, but his happiness was not to last long. He came down with the chills and fever. The men liked the kid, so when they were in Tantie they asked Doc Anner for some medicine for him. She gave them some calomel with instructions that he should be given all of the white powder that could be stacked on a dime, followed by a good dose of Epsom salts or castor oil, and then nothing to eat or drink till the chills and fever were gone.

"She handed them a little sack of white powder and added, 'Be sure you tell the sisters that it is very important that they give him the right amount,' and added, 'The first time I'm out that way I'll stop by and check on him.'

"It was payday and, as usual, the fishermen got drunk, which dulled their senses about the boy's needs. When they got back to the lake, Si was seriously ill. The DoseDo Sisters were blurry eyed from trying to drown their fears with moonshine. They were still aware of the urgency to give the boy the medicine, though, and ramshackled the place looking for a dime. Si started shaking again with another chill, and one of the sisters said, 'We'll just have to use a nickel.'

"The other sister reasoned, 'But that will be only half enough, and Doc Anner said it was very important to give him the proper amount.'

"'That's right, and he is one more sick boy!'

"'But iffen we don't do something and do it fast, he's not gonna make it.'

"Both of them started crying, then one wiped her eyes and said, 'Sister, I found another nickel! Two nickels make a dime. That'll work.' "With that decision made, they measured out all the calomel that they could heap onto the two nickels. What a blessing that their hands shook and much of it was lost before they were able to give it to the boy. But even so, Si was overdosed and was lingering, closer to death than life, when the doctor, returning from an emergency, stopped to check on him. When she saw him, she thought that his symptoms were those of someone who was overdosed. As soon as the sisters explained what they had done, the doctor went to work to counteract it. She was able to save him, although his health was broken. Si was never again able to work with the seine crews. Some folks thought that the incident affected his mind as well as his body, but all agreed that his fiddle playing was still superb.

"Of course, all this happened long before I knew him. My earliest recollection of Uncle Si was his sincere testimony at a Thanksgiving Day celebration, when he said, 'I am most thankful that the DoseDo Sisters had two nickels when I had the chills and fever.'

"I had heard the story of the overdosing so I thought he was simple-minded when I heard him say it the first time, and I was sure that his mind was warped when I heard him repeat it year after year. But I learned to like Uncle Si, and the year I was sixteen, MaryBeth stirred my emotions so that I was not only in love with her but filled with empathy for him. With no thought of embarrassing the man, I spoke up: 'Uncle Si, why are you thankful that they had two nickels when they almost killed you with them?'

"PaPa looked at me and I could feel a reprimand coming, which would be bad enough anytime, but the thought of being dressed down in front of my new love made me wish I could find a gopher hole so I could crawl in and pull the dirt in behind me.

"But Uncle Si looked at me and with a twinkle in his eye said, 'But, Charles, you ain't given a thought ter what would've happened iffen they hadn't had a dime or two nickels and had used ten pennies.'

"A smile replaced the scowl on PaPa's face. He walked over and gave Uncle Si a hearty pat on his back as he said, 'Amen, Brother. Amen!'"

Telling time: 10–12 minutes
Audience: 4th grade–adult

I want to acknowledge and thank my cousins Ray and Jeanne for their contribution to this story.

Guest Ghosts

The Spanish galleon lurched like a wounded swan on the darkening Gulf waters. The pirate ship, silhouetted against the sinking sun, slid alongside like a vulture, and a swarm of sordid men, eager to finish the fight, stormed onboard. The outnumbered Spaniards fought gallantly until all were strewn like trash over the deck. The pirates, now eager for their loot, poured down the gangway with Captain Gaspar striding ahead. When he reached the closed stateroom door, he kicked it open, then stopped, frozen in his tracks. As the men stared into the twilight gloom, silence spread until only the lapping of the water was heard. There before them was a señora whose classical beauty seemed to brighten the room. In the face of death, her regal bearing was as obvious as the white lace mantilla that cascaded over her blue-black hair.

Gaspar broke the silence with a bellow. "I swear I'll cut the heart out of any man who touches her."

The men slowly returned to the deck and collapsed among the cadavers and gore. Later, Gaspar broke the silence with his orders to board ship, and from their ship the men watched, in amazement, as the notorious, swashbuckling Gaspar courteously led the señora to the deck. He tenderly placed her violin in her arms, and then, with a sweeping bow, Gaspar backed to the rail and jumped over to the waiting boat. After the order to set sail rang clear, Gaspar stood in the stern of the receding vessel and watched as the white mantilla rippled in the evening breezes.

The clear tones of the violin stole over the waters—violin music that is still heard off Florida's Gulf Coast during the moonlit nights of May. But few, indeed, live to tell it when they linger to listen to the violin music during the dark nights of October. It is then that the phantom ship appears, disappears, and reappears, with the long-drawn tones of the violin coming from her deck. She is crossing the Gulf's troubled waters to bring winter tourist ghosts to old Florida Cracker houses.

Before you flip your calendar to November, there's always a guest ghost in every pantry and two upon the stairs. There are three guests in the attic and four sitting on the chairs. There are five in the kitchen and six out in the hall. There are seven ghosts on the ceiling and eight upon the wall. There are nine guests in the parlor, doing what ghosts always do! And ten ghosts at your back and all of them shouting, "BOO!"

Telling time: 4–5 minutes
Audience: 5th grade–adult

The Season's Seasoning

W ell, now, I'll tell you, down in Palm Beach a few years ago, a Mr. and Mrs. Small were a couple, along about sixty, who had plenty of money. They'd worked hard during their lives, had had many lucky breaks, and had pinched here and pinched there until they'd sort of pinched themselves. They had become a selfish, hard-hearted couple. They lived in a big mansion because they wanted folks to know they were rich. They had gardeners, maids, cooks, a butler, a chauffeur, and other trappings that went with having money, but even so they were not happy.

The year I had in mind telling you about, Christmas came along and about five o'clock in the afternoon, Mr. and Mrs. Small set down to their Christmas dinner. There was crystal a-sparklin', silver a-shinin', and an assortment of spoons to do the spoonin' with, and all sorts of other eatin' gear. The tablecloth and big dinner napkins had fancy air holes all embroidered in them. The couple sat there just as stiff as two frozen flagpoles, Mr. Small at one end of the table and Mrs. Small at the other. They were so far apart they needed to wave their napkins at each other to make sure they were both there.

Well, the butler commenced to serve. They had soup and a mite of this and a speck of that.

Mr. Small said, "This soup ain't hot enough. Heat it up!"

Mrs. Small said, "James, put an extra plate under the soup so it won't mar the table."

And then Mr. Small took a sip of the reheated soup. It burned his tongue, and he let out a stream of words that I won't repeat.

When the turkey was served, Mr. Small thought the dressing wasn't seasoned enough, and Mrs. Small thought it was seasoned too much. And then a mite of holly dropped off the chandelier and got on the plate, and Mr. Small bit into it before he saw what it was. Well, they kept a-nibblin' and a-fussin' and a-fussin' and a-nibblin'.

After a while, Mrs. Small looked up and saw a ragamuffin about twelve years old with his nose flattened up against the window and his eyes stretched wide. That woman came out of her chair like she'd been stung by a whole colony of fire ants. She rang the buzzer for James. When the butler came in, Mrs. Small yelled, "Get that guttersnipe off the grounds. Throw him over the fence. I've told you for the last time to keep all the gates locked."

"Yes, madam," said James and went out the pantry door.

Well, the Smalls kept on a-pickin' at the turkey and each other till, when they got up from the table, they were feeling lower than a snake's belly. Mrs. Small went upstairs to get away from Mr. Small, and Mr. Small went into the library to get away from Mrs. Small.

Then, for the first time in years, Mr. Small decided to light a fire himself. He started into the kitchen to get a match. Well, sir, when he opened the door, he thought he was seeing ghosts. There were the butler and the butler's wife sitting down to their Christmas dinner at the kitchen table—giggling and having a great time—and right between them was the ragamuffin Mrs. Small had ordered the butler to throw over the fence. As soon as the butler and his wife saw Mr. Small, the smiles left their faces for they figured they'd get their walking tickets. But they offered no apologies. The boy bent a bit further over his plate of victuals, and all of them went right on eating. Mr. Small looked at them a minute and then went over to get the match. He took his time doing it, though, and sort of peeked out the corners of his eyes. He wasn't in any hurry to leave the kitchen; it felt so warm and comfortable. He fumbled for the match and just sort of stood there.

Pretty soon the boy turned to him and said, "Mister, this here food is awful good. Ain't you goin' ter eat some?"

For the first time in months, a smile came to the corners of Mr. Small's mouth and his stomach commenced to feel empty. And in no time he was sitting down at the kitchen table with a dishtowel tucked in his collar and his sleeves rolled up, spoonin' up victuals with the butler, the butler's wife, and with the boy, whose name was Tom.

Along with the victuals came some funny stories too, some that Mr. Small had known for ages but hadn't thought of for years. Right in the middle of a big laugh, the kitchen door opened and in came Mrs. Small. Her nose was stuck up in the air like a weathercock on top of a cupola, and when she saw her husband sitting down at the kitchen table with the butler, his wife, and that ragamuffin, she stood there dumbfounded.

But she'd commenced her married life doing her own cooking, and the warmth of the stove and the smell of the pots and pans kinda got under her skin, and when Mr. Small looked up and said with a chuckle, "Come on in, honey, sit down and have something to eat," she did. For a little while she wasn't all thawed out, but it wasn't long before she'd forgot about trying to be something she wasn't and started spooning up victuals along with the rest of them.

Well, sir, the old gentleman bent over his plate with a lump in his throat and a funny feeling in his heart. A tear or two dropped onto the dressing, and it seemed like the tears seasoned the dressing so it was the best dressing he'd ever tasted in his life. When it was all over and they'd wrapped up some gifts and let little Tom open them, the hands on the clock said eleven, and Mr. Small called the chauffeur to take Tom and his presents back to where he lived.

As Tom started to leave, Mr. Small said to him, "I wonder if you'd come back for New Year's Eve."

"I sure will," said Tom, beaming all over, "but it's kind of far away, ain't it?"

For just a moment the old gentleman thought, and then he said, "No, Tommy, we have New Year's early in our house. We're going to have it tomorrow."

"Then I'll be here," Tom said as he ran out to get into an automobile for the first time in his life.

And so the Smalls had New Year's the day after Christmas, and I heard they enjoyed it so much that they had Christmas one day, New Year's the next, and Thanksgiving the next for some time. And later, after little Tom grew up, every time he came home from college, the Smalls had Christmas every day.

So, I tell you, if you want to season the season, just invite someone in who is not going to have a Christmas dinner, and you'll find that you've added the secret seasoning for the best dressing you've ever tasted.

Telling time: 10–11 minutes
Audience: 3rd grade–adult

Here's a good, tellable story that must have been a spin-off of the successful "Bringing Up Father" cartoon strip and its real-life characters. I heard it more than fifty years ago and don't recall ever hearing the title. This is my version, which I've added to my telling repertoire.

Index

If you enjoyed reading this book, here are some other books from Pineapple Press on related topics. For a complete catalog, write to: Pineapple Press, P.O. Box 3889, Sarasota, FL 34230 or call 1-800-PINEAPL (746-3275). Or visit our website at www.pineapplepress.com.

200 Quick Looks at Florida History by James C. Clark. Covers 10,000 years of Florida history in 200 brief history lessons. A boon to students, newcomers, and those who simply want to learn more about Florida and its rich and varied history, this book is packed with unusual and little-known facts and stories. ISBN 1-56164-200-2 (pb)

Alligator Tales by Kevin M. McCarthy. True and tongue-in-cheek accounts of alligators and the people who have hunted them, been attacked by them, and tried to save them from extinction. Filled with amusing black-and-white photographs and punctuated by a section of full-color photos by award-winning *Gainesville Sun* photographer John Moran. ISBN 1-56164-158-8 (pb)

The Florida Chronicles by Stuart B. McIver. A series offering true-life sagas of the notable and notorious characters throughout history who have given Florida its distinctive flavor. **Volume 1**: *Dreamers, Schemers and Scalawags* ISBN 1-56164-155-3 (pb); **Volume 2**: *Murder in the Tropics* ISBN 1-56164-079-4 (hb); **Volume 3**: *Touched by the Sun* ISBN 1-56164-206-1 (hb)

The Florida Keys by John Viele. The trials and successes of the Keys pioneers are brought to life in this series, which recounts tales of early pioneer life and life at sea. **Volume 1**: *A History of the Pioneers* ISBN 1-56164-101-4 (hb); **Volume 2**: *True Stories of the Perilous Straits* ISBN 1-56164-179-0 (hb); **Volume 3**: *The Wreckers* ISBN 1-56164-219-3 (hb)

Florida Portrait by Jerrell Shofner. Packed with hundreds of photos, this word-and-picture album traces the history of Florida from the Paleo-Indians to the rampant growth of the late twentieth century. ISBN 1-56164-121-9 (pb)

Florida's Past Volumes 1, 2, and 3 by Gene Burnett. Collected essays from Burnett's "Florida's Past" columns in *Florida Trend* magazine, plus some original writings not found elsewhere. Burnett's easygoing style and his sometimes surprising choice of topics make history good reading. **Volume 1** ISBN 1-56164-115-4 (pb); **Volume 2** ISBN 1-56164-139-1 (pb); **Volume 3** ISBN 1-56164-117-0 (pb)

Legends of the Seminoles by Betty Mae Jumper. This collection of rich spoken tales—written down for the first time—impart valuable lessons about living in harmony with nature and about why the world is the way it is. Each story is illustrated with an original painting by Guy LaBree. ISBN 1-56164-033-6 (hb); ISBN 1-56164-040-9 (pb)

Sandspun collected by Annette Bruce and J. Stephen Brooks. A collection of tales rich with homespun humor, charm, and wisdom, all told with flair by some of Florida's best storytellers. You'll find ghost stories, tall tales, nature stories, morality tales, and stories that will have you in stitches! Great for reading aloud to children and adults alike. ISBN 1-56164-242-8 (hb); ISBN 1-56164-243-6 (pb)

Tellable Cracker Tales collected by Annette Bruce. Memorable characters from Florida history come alive in these folktales and legends, tall tales, and gator tales. Pull up your favorite chair and a few listeners and start your own storytelling tradition with the gems in this collection. ISBN 1-56164-100-6 (hb); ISBN 1-56164-094-8 (pb)